DAN GUTMAN

FLASHBACK FOUR

FOUR

THE TITANIC MISSION

SCHOLASTIC INC.

ISBN 978-1-338-21270-9

12 11 10 9 8 7 6 5 4 3 2   17 18 19 20 21 22

Printed in the U.S.A.   40

First Scholastic printing, September 2017

Typography by Carla Weise

TO NINA, SAM, AND EMMA

There is nothing that man can build that nature cannot destroy, and far as he may advance in might and knowledge and cunning, her blind strength will always be more than his match.

—Filson Young, *Titanic*

Special thanks to the people who helped me with this project: Ray Dimetrosky, David Lubar, Craig Provorny, Nina Wallace, and Howard Wolf.

INTRODUCTION

IT WAS TWENTY MINUTES BEFORE MIDNIGHT when steel touched ice.

The date: April 14, 1912.

The place: the north Atlantic Ocean, about 370 miles southeast of Newfoundland.

It was cold outside. So cold. As cold as ice.

The ocean was flat and calm that night, almost like a sheet of glass. The largest ship in the world at the time—the *Titanic*—had nearly completed its maiden voyage. It sliced through the water at top speed, close to twenty-four miles per hour.

The sky was clear, cloudless, and almost moonless,

except for a tiny sliver. But the stars were bright and sometimes shooting. So peaceful. It must have been tempting to take one's eye off the distant horizon and gaze up at the star show above.

Maybe that's what happened. Maybe the lookout glanced up and saw a shooting star. He couldn't take his eyes off it. And then, when he returned his gaze to the horizon moments later, he saw it directly in front of him—an enormous mountain of ice.

In Greek mythology, the Titans were a race of giant gods with incredible strength who ruled the Golden Age. That's how the *Titanic* got its name.

It would seem like no contest—frozen water versus hard steel. But it was the steel that broke, not the ice.

The iceberg towered sixty feet high, and that was just the part of it that was above the waterline. It was eight times larger *below* the surface, and four times the size of the *Titanic* steaming directly toward it—a *million* tons of ice.

Everything happened so fast after that. The lookout turned around and frantically rang the emergency bell three times.

"Hard starboard!" somebody on the bridge shouted almost immediately.

But it was far too late. It's not easy to turn around

a vessel that's nine hundred feet long and weighs over forty-six *thousand* tons. It takes time, and that was one thing in short supply. *Titanic* was only a quarter mile away from the iceberg and closing fast.

It's easy to say now, but it probably would have been better if the *Titanic* hadn't turned at all. It should have just rammed the iceberg head-on. The front of the ship was designed to take a hit. It might have survived the damage. The sides of the ship were much more fragile.

Just thirty-seven seconds after the emergency bell rang, steel touched ice on the front right side of *Titanic*—the starboard side. The impact was ten feet above the keel, but well below the waterline.

There was no crash. No jolt. It appeared to be a glancing blow. A little bump. Harmless. *Titanic* didn't even stop moving forward. The iceberg didn't break apart. It was like . . . two ships passing in the night.

But the hull of the *Titanic*—like any large ship—was made of hundreds of overlapping steel plates, each of them just an inch and a half thick. These plates were held in place by iron rivets. The rivets were small, just an inch thick and three inches long. When ice touched steel, something had to give.

It was the rivets. Iron isn't as strong as steel. One at

a time the rivets popped off. *Pop. Pop. Pop.* The heads of the rivets had been sliced off, like mushrooms.

The hull didn't open up like a zipper or a can opener, the way it has sometimes been described. Without rivets to hold them in place, the steel plates that lined the ship were roughly shoved aside, like a toddler ripping the wrapping paper off a birthday present.

Water gushed in the gash, four hundred tons of it a minute. The sixteen "watertight" compartments that lined the hull began to fill.

Only some of the passengers on board heard the rumbling, grinding noise below deck. Most of them were asleep and didn't notice a thing.

And then, just like that, it was over. The iceberg floated on by as if nothing unusual had happened. It was chipped in a few places but none the worse for wear.

In less than ten seconds, the damage had been done to *Titanic.* That's all it took. The "unsinkable" ship was fatally injured. And the unthinkable was about to happen.

THE FLASHBACK FOUR

TO TELL THIS STORY THE WAY IT SHOULD BE TOLD, we need to go back, or, I should say, *forward* in time.

The story begins in the present day, in the left field bleachers at Fenway Park in Boston, Massachusetts. The Red Sox are playing the Yankees, but the ball game is secondary to what's going on in the stands.

Sitting in the front row above Fenway's famous Green Monster are four sixth-grade students. You already met them if you read a book called *Flashback Four: The Lincoln Project.* If you haven't read it, you really should. If you *have* read it, all the better.

It's impossible and really unfair, of course, to sum up a human being in just a few sentences. But at the same time, you don't want to sit through page after page of character description. You'll get to know these young people better as the story goes on. But for now we're all busy, so here goes . . .

Luke: A big white kid from the streets of Dorchester. He's got a touch of ADD and a heart of gold.

Julia: A prep school blonde who likes money, clothes, and taking risks, maybe a little too much.

David: A tall, thin African American kid who likes to laugh but knows when to get serious.

Isabel: A studious kid originally from the Dominican Republic who plays by the rules, and expects to be rewarded for it.

Two boys. Two girls. They call themselves the Flashback Four. They didn't know each other until quite recently. They go to separate schools. But they bonded, as often happens when people are thrown into a life-or-death situation together. In surviving the Lincoln Project they became friends, and they'd decided to get together to talk about their future . . . and the past.

Luke and David are serious Red Sox fans, but that's not how the Flashback Four found themselves in

Fenway Park that day. They got the tickets from Julia's father, a wealthy Boston hedge fund manager.

I know what you're thinking. There can't be a lot of money in managing hedges. But Julia's dad did quite well for himself and had season tickets. Taking his wealthy clients to Fenway was good for business. He had four tickets he wasn't using on this particular day and offered them to Julia.

This is a girl who doesn't know the difference between a foul ball and a grand slam. But she knew the boys would appreciate it, and she thought it would be a nice way to get the group together after they got back from their first adventure.

"Free tickets to see the Sox play the Yankees!" Luke said, high-fiving David as they found their seats. "It doesn't get much better than this."

"Baseball is such a *bore*." Julia yawned. "What do they have to eat around here?"

Neither team scored in the first inning, but the Flashback Four weren't paying much attention to the game anyway. They were still recovering from what had happened at Gettysburg.

To put it simply, they had been recruited by a billionaire—Miss Chris Zandergoth—who had earned her fortune developing an online dating site called

Findamate. She spent a big chunk of that fortune creating an interactive smartboard that could function as a time-traveling device.

It was simply called the Board. If you think the smartboard in *your* school is high-tech, you ain't seen nothin'. This was a smarter board. Don't even try to understand the technology. It's for super techies.

Anyway, Miss Zandergoth sent the Flashback Four to 1863 with a mission—to take a photograph of Abraham Lincoln delivering the Gettysburg Address. Miss Z, as she is called, has an obsession with photos of historical events, and especially historical events that have never been photographed before. There is no existing photo of Lincoln giving that speech. Go ahead, look it up. Or just take my word for it.

Luke, Julia, Isabel, and David *were* able to witness the Gettysburg Address in person, but unfortunately they were *not* able to bring back a photo of Lincoln delivering it. In fact, they were attacked and jailed, and poor Julia even had the misfortune to step in a pile of 1863 dog poop. To tell you the truth, the Flashback Four were lucky to get back to the present day with their lives. If you want the full story, again, read the book.

The Red Sox took the field to start the second inning. Luke had just come back to the seats with hot dogs for everybody.

"Y'know," Isabel said as she took a bite, "with the Board, we could travel to *any* moment in time and take a picture of it."

"Obviously," David said.

"Where do you think Miss Z will send us next?" Luke asked.

The possibilities were endless. The first photograph ever taken was in 1826. So no photos exist of *anything* that happened before that year. They could go back to Christmas night of 1776 and photograph George Washington with his troops, crossing the Delaware to launch a surprise attack on the British army at Trenton. Or they could go back to 1510 and photograph Michelangelo as he painted his masterpiece on the ceiling of the Sistine Chapel. Or they could go back to prehistoric times and snap a photo of a dinosaur.

"You know what would be cool?" Isabel said. "We could take a picture of the Wright Brothers flying the first airplane at Kitty Hawk, North Carolina."

"I'm pretty sure there's already a picture of that," Luke said. "I think I saw it in a book once."

Luke was right. Orville and Wilbur Wright very carefully documented their experiments with flying machines, and they had a member of the Kill Devil Hills Lifesaving Station snap a photo just as Orville lifted off the ground for the first time on December 17, 1903. The flight lasted all of twelve seconds. It was one of the most famous photographs of the twentieth century. So there was no point in trying to take *that* picture.

It only took a few seconds for Julia to find it on her smartphone. . . .

The first batter for the Yankees grounded out, and the second one singled up the middle.

The Flashback Four discussed a few other possibilities for photos. Amazingly, nobody had thought to take a photograph of generals Ulysses S. Grant and Robert E. Lee signing the agreement to end the Civil War. There was no photograph of Amelia Earhart crash-landing her plane on a remote island in the Pacific Ocean, of course. A photo of the Founding Fathers signing the Declaration of Independence would be amazing. Many famous events in history can only be imagined from paintings that were made of them.

As the next Yankee stepped up to the plate, a message flashed on the scoreboard. None of the Flashback Four noticed it at first. . . .

DID YOU KNOW ...

the message read,

FENWAY PARK IS THE OLDEST MAJOR LEAGUE BALLPARK IN AMERICA?

"Who cares?" muttered Julia, glancing up at the scoreboard as she took a bite of her hot dog.

IT OPENED ON APRIL 20, 1912.

"Big deal," muttered Julia.

**HERE ARE A FEW OTHER FAMOUS EVENTS THAT
HAPPENED IN 1912....**
- **JANUARY: The Republic of China was established**
- **FEBRUARY: Arizona became the 48th state**
- **MARCH: The Dixie Cup was invented**
- **APRIL: The *TITANIC* sank in the Atlantic Ocean**

The word *Titanic* caught Isabel's eye as she glanced up at the scoreboard. The story of the *Titanic* was one of those things that just about everybody knew, even though it happened so long ago and it isn't taught in schools. It was one of the most famous events of the twentieth century. Isabel had seen the 1997 movie *Titanic* during a sleepover at a friend's house. She nudged Julia, who Googled the word *Titanic* on her smartphone.

"It says here that the *Titanic* sank on April 15, 1912," she said. "That was just five days before this ballpark opened."

Nobody said anything for a minute or two. The Yankee batter took a couple pitches out of the strike zone, and then grounded into a double play, throwing the Red Sox fans into a frenzy. David turned to Luke.

"Are you thinking what I'm thinking?" he asked.

"I think I'm thinking *exactly* what you're thinking," Luke replied. "Is there a photo of the *Titanic* sinking?"

Isabel looked it up on her phone.

"No," she reported. "It says here that there are plenty of pictures of the *Titanic* before it set sail, but no photos of it actually sinking."

"Why not?" asked Julia. "They had cameras in 1912."

"All the cameras that were on board probably went down with the ship," David guessed, "and the people in the lifeboats couldn't bring anything with them. They were just trying to stay alive."

"It was women and children first," Isabel noted. "Maybe in those days, women weren't allowed to *use* cameras. We couldn't even vote until 1920."

The Yankee batter struck out to end the inning, causing the crowd to erupt in cheers, but none of the Flashback Four were paying attention to the game anymore.

"Can you imagine how cool it would be to sail on the *Titanic*?" asked Luke.

"I would do it," Julia said. "We would get to hobnob with all those rich society people."

"Count me out, guys," Isabel announced. "Too dangerous for me."

She had pulled out her own phone and was scrolling through various websites about the *Titanic*. She learned that the ship was going too fast that night. The captain ignored multiple warnings about icebergs in the area. The rivets holding the ship together should have been made of steel instead of iron. There weren't enough lifeboats for all the passengers. The lookout didn't even have binoculars, because they were locked in a locker and nobody had the key! So many things had gone wrong, and fifteen hundred people had died.

"What, do you want to spend your whole life staring at a cell phone?" David told her. "Come on. We could do this. YOLO. You only live once."

"And you only *die* once!" Isabel replied. "Are you crazy? It would be a suicide mission! Most of the people on the *Titanic died*, you know. We almost got killed just going to Gettysburg. Do you think we're going to survive on a ship that's going to sink?"

"Yeah, we'll survive," Luke said calmly. "Because we have something none of those *Titanic* passengers had."

"What?" asked Isabel.

"The Board," Luke said, looking at her. "As soon

as we snap the picture, Miss Z will zap us back home. Easy peasy. We're not going to die. You don't even have to get your feet wet."

"Hmmm," Isabel said. "I didn't think of it that way."

ANOTHER CHANCE

THE RED SOX ENDED UP WINNING THE GAME THAT day, but even Luke—the most diehard fan of them all— wasn't able to get that excited about it. He couldn't stop thinking about traveling back to April 15, 1912, to take a photo of the *Titanic* before it slipped under the water. After much discussion—and a good amount of ice cream and popcorn—Luke, David, and Julia convinced Isabel to go along with what they had dubbed "the *Titanic* Mission."

As soon as school let out the next day, the Flashback Four gathered at 200 Clarendon Street in downtown Boston to discuss the idea with Miss Zandergoth.

"Okay, let's do this thing," Luke said when Julia showed up a few minutes after the others.

The John Hancock Tower is a sixty-story sky-scraper with hundreds of business offices of all kinds. As they pushed through the revolving door into the lobby, all four members of the Flashback Four felt more confident than they had before the Lincoln Project. They knew their way around this place. Only a few people were waiting for the elevator. Isabel pushed the button.

"That doesn't do anything, you know," David told her.

"What do you mean it doesn't do anything?" she replied. "Of *course* it does something. When you push the button, it calls the elevator."

"Nah, the elevators are programmed to go up and down at predetermined times," David told her. "It's gonna come whether you press the button or not."

"What?!" asked Julia. "You're nuts. If the button doesn't do anything, what's the point of having it here?"

"They just put the button there to give people the feeling that they're in control," David informed her. "It's the same thing with those signals at intersections that tell you when to walk across the street. Those buttons don't do anything either. It's all a sham."

"Where'd you hear *that*?" asked Luke.

"I know stuff, okay?" David told them. "This is common knowledge, you guys."

Whatever made it happen, a few seconds later the door opened and the Flashback Four stepped inside the elevator. Julia pressed the button for the twenty-third floor.

"I suppose *this* button doesn't do anything either?" she asked.

"I'm looking into that," David said mysteriously. "I have my doubts."

There was only one office on the twenty-third floor—Pasture Company. Below the logo, a sign read,

IF I DON'T SEE YOU IN THE FUTURE,
I'LL SEE YOU IN THE PASTURE.

Julia, Isabel, David, and Luke strode up to the front desk.

"Well, we weren't expecting to see the four of you back here so quickly," said the smiling receptionist, Mrs. Ella Vader. "Aren't you kids supposed to be in school right now?"

"It's after four o'clock," Isabel said. "School is out."

"So it is," said Mrs. Vader. "Time flies, doesn't it?"

"Can we speak with Miss Z?" asked David.

"Gee, I wish you had called ahead," replied Mrs. Vader. "Miss Z is in the middle of something very important. But let me see if I can squeeze you in."

The kids took seats in the waiting area while Mrs. Vader buzzed her boss on the intercom. Luke got up to examine the framed photos covering the walls: Neil Armstrong standing on the surface of the moon. Harry Truman gleefully holding up a newspaper with the headline "Dewey Defeats Truman." Martin Luther King, Jr. delivering his "I Have a Dream" speech at the Lincoln Memorial. Several American presidents taking the oath of office. It was a living history lesson.

A few minutes later, Mrs. Vader motioned for the kids to enter the inner office. Luke opened the door and went in first.

Miss Z was at her desk, sitting in her wheelchair, still talking on the phone. She motioned for the kids to take seats. They looked at the historical photos all over the walls while she finished up her call.

"What do you mean it can't be done?" Miss Z just about shouted into the phone. "Of *course* it can be done. And it *must*! What else do you people have to do with your time? The fate of the planet is at stake!"

Miss Z slammed down the phone and turned to face the kids.

"Well, hello," she said cheerfully.

"*What* can't be done?" Isabel asked.

"Some dope at NASA tells me that it wouldn't be cost effective to launch metallic shades into outer space."

"Why would you want to launch metallic shades into space?" asked Julia.

"You've heard about global warming?" Miss Z asked. "Climate change? Well, if we placed a line of shades in orbit around the Earth, it would reduce the amount of sunlight hitting the planet by at least two percent. Bingo! Climate change is solved. Simple!"

"That's possible?" Isabel asked.

"Of *course* it's possible!" Miss Z replied. "Anything is possible if you have the right technology and enough money to build stuff."

"Couldn't we reverse climate change if we just stopped burning fossil fuels and switched to renewable sources of energy?" asked Isabel. "Isn't that a more logical solution?"

"You think people are going to stop driving cars?" asked Miss Z with a snort. "Do you think people are going to stop taking flights to visit grandma and grandpa on Thanksgiving? Space sunshades would be the perfect technological fix to an urgent problem, and we wouldn't have to make any sacrifices or lower our standard of living. And it would be *fast*." Miss Z snapped her fingers, as if to show how fast her solution to climate change would be.

David glanced at Luke. Up until now, he'd thought Miss Z was a genius. It took a genius to develop the Board to send people back and forth through time. But launching sunshades into outer space? That just sounded like a crackpot idea.

Mrs. Vader poked her head in the door and asked if she should bring in tea for everyone.

"That won't be necessary, Ella," said Miss Z. "We won't be long. What can I do for you kids today?"

"We have an idea," Isabel said.

"Well you know me," replied Miss Z. "I'm all about ideas. Tell me more."

"We have an idea for another mission to go on," David said. "An idea involving the Board."

"Oh." Miss Z cast her eyes downward for a moment. "*That* kind of idea. I'm sorry. Umm, I forgot to tell you kids something."

"What?" David asked.

"You're fired," she said matter-of-factly.

"What?!" the kids all shouted as one.

"Look, I'd like to be diplomatic about this," Miss

Z said, looking each of them in the eye as she spoke, "but life is short, and I've got no time for ambiguity. And if you don't know what ambiguity means, go look it up. You all have smartphones. My point is, I gave you kids a job to do when I sent you to Gettysburg, and you didn't do it. You didn't complete the mission. I was deeply disappointed."

She rolled over to the wall of photos. It was filled, except for one empty space where a picture was missing.

"I assigned you to take a photo of Abraham Lincoln delivering the Gettysburg Address," Miss Z reminded them. "As you know, no such photo exists. And no photo *will* exist because *you* screwed up. And no, you can't have a do-over. The technology of the Board doesn't have the capability to send you back to the same place twice. So there will *never* be a photo of Lincoln making that speech. And it's your fault."

"But—" Luke tried to explain, but Miss Z cut him off.

"It was a simple job," she continued. "You failed, and I don't tolerate failure. I wouldn't be where I am today if I allowed my underlings to fail more than once. When employees mess up, I get rid of them. This is not a game. This is very important to me. I need to work with people I can count on."

The Flashback Four certainly weren't expecting this kind of criticism. They had never heard such blunt talk, and they were shocked into silence. Well, except for Luke.

"You sent us to Gettysburg on the wrong *day*, remember?" he said quietly, but firmly. "So *you* screwed up too. I bet we would have been able to get the picture of Lincoln if you hadn't typed the wrong date into the computer."

Miss Z looked at Luke. She wasn't used to being challenged, especially by someone so young.

But Luke was right, of course, and Miss Z knew it. Because she had typed 11/18/1863 instead of 11/19/1863, the Flashback Four arrived in Gettysburg the day *before* Lincoln gave his famous speech. So they'd had to find a place to sleep that night. They'd had to feed themselves, and she hadn't given them any money. They'd encountered all kinds of problems they wouldn't have had to deal with if they'd arrived at Gettysburg on the right day.

Miss Z was not the kind of person who liked to hear about her *own* failures. But on some level, she admired Luke for speaking his mind and not backing down.

"Sending you to Gettysburg one day earlier had no

bearing on completing your mission," she told him. "You still could have gotten the shot. I was counting on you for that picture to add to my collection. I'm sorry, but that's the way it is. If you'll excuse me, I'm very busy."

So much for the time-traveling career of the Flashback Four. They had been given one mission, and they'd blown it. Miss Z looked down at the paperwork on her desk, as if David, Luke, Isabel, and Julia didn't exist anymore.

One by one, the kids got up to leave. They all felt humiliated, and Isabel was on the verge of tears. She was a straight-A student. She had been counting on using her time-traveling experience to help get into a good college in a few years. It might help her get a job down the line. Impressing adults was important to Isabel, and she wasn't used to being told that she was incompetent.

When he opened the door, David stopped and turned around.

"It wasn't all our fault," he said to Miss Z. "You messed up too. You should give us another chance."

"And risk another failure?" Miss Z said without looking up from her paperwork. "Time is money, young man."

"But we have a good idea," Luke said. "You didn't even let us explain it to you."

Miss Z sighed and looked up from her paperwork. "What *is* it?" she asked, as if she really didn't care what it was.

This time it was Julia who stepped forward. "I think I can sum up our idea with one word," she said. "Titanic."

Miss Z put both of her hands behind her neck and leaned back in her wheelchair. "I'm listening," she said.

David closed the door. The Flashback Four gathered around Miss Z's desk once again. They had done some homework to prepare for this moment.

"The *Titanic* was the largest ocean liner in the world," Luke explained. "On its first voyage, *boom*, it sideswipes an iceberg. The iceberg rips a hole in the ship, and it goes down. April 15, 1912. Five days before Fenway Park opened. Over a thousand innocent people die."

"Fifteen hundred," added Isabel.

"I know the story," Miss Z said. "Everybody knows the story. So what?"

"There's *no* picture of it," David said. He went over and pointed to the empty space on Miss Z's wall. "Imagine a photo right *here* of the great *Titanic* just before it goes under. How cool would that be?"

"It was one of the most historic events of the twentieth century," Luke added, "and there's no picture of it. Such a shame."

No photo, no proof. If it weren't for the famous movie, it would sound like a legend to the next generation of kids. Nobody would even know it had ever happened.

"And we could fix that," Isabel said. "We could take that picture."

Miss Z looked at the empty space on the wall again and imagined the image that would fill that space. Her eyes grew larger.

"It *is* a compelling idea," she said. "I must admit, it would make a marvelous addition to my collection."

Miss Z had long dreamed of creating a museum devoted to photos of the most important events in history. That was what she hoped would be her legacy when she was gone. She didn't want to be remembered just because she created a silly dating website.

Miss Z knew a thing or two about human nature in the internet age. Few people are willing to take the time to read history books or even watch videos about the events that shaped our world. It's so much easier to just turn on a TV and watch the Kardashians or some other nonsense. But a picture—as they say—is worth a thousand words. A still photo that sums up an event can be appreciated almost instantly by anyone.

People would come from all over the world to see her photography museum. It would be a great way to educate children about history. And it would be children, of course, who would determine the course of history in the future.

"Are you *sure* there's no existing photo of the *Titanic* sinking?" Miss Z asked the group.

"We looked it up," Julia replied. "There's nothing."

"Okay." Miss Z sighed. "I'll give you one more chance."

GETTING READY

"MOM AND DAD, IS IT OKAY IF I TRAVEL BACK IN time to 1912 so I can take a ride on the *Titanic* and shoot a picture of it just as it's about to sink?"

Right. There was no way in a million years that anybody's mother or father was going to give them permission to go on such a crazy mission. No parent would ever believe it could even happen, much less approve of it.

So Julia did what she always does—she never even showed her parents the permission slip that Miss Z had given her to get signed. Julia simply forged her father's signature and brought it back without telling him.

Isabel wasn't quite so dishonest. She told her

parents that she needed their permission to go on a "historic boat tour." Technically, she wasn't lying. Or at least that was what she *told* herself. Her parents figured it would be a tour of the USS *Constitution* or one of the other famous ships moored in the Charlestown Navy Yard nearby, and they signed the permission slip gladly. Neither of them had finished high school, and they desperately wanted Isabel to go to college someday. Anything that appeared to be educational always got a quick okay in the Alvarez household.

David had never been a good liar. Every time he tried to get away with something by lying about it, he got caught. So he figured out a creative technique to get away with things he shouldn't be doing—he would tell the absolute truth and hope his parents would assume he was joking.

"Remember that rich white lady who invented a magic smartboard and sent me back to see Lincoln deliver the Gettysburg Address?" he asked his mother. "Well, now she wants to put me on the *Titanic* just before it sinks."

"Very funny," his mother replied, as she took a pen and signed the permission slip. "Just keep your grades up, mister."

Luke knew that his parents were both busy working

multiple jobs, and neither of them had the time or energy to go over all the forms, slips, and announcements he brought home from school every few days.

"Here, sign this," he said when his father came home from work and flopped on the couch with his remote control.

"What is it?"

"I don't know," Luke replied. "It's just some school garbage."

His father signed the paper.

On the first mission of the Flashback Four, Miss Z did all the Gettysburg research herself and simply told the kids what to do and where to go. This time, she felt they should be more personally invested in the mission. After all, it was their idea. She told the kids that she expected them to do some of the research themselves. So when they gathered on the twenty-third floor of the Hancock Tower two days later, the kids were prepared.

"So what have you got?" she asked as she collected their signed permission slips.

Isabel and Luke stood up. Each of them held a page of notes.

"We decided to learn about what the world was

like back in 1912, so we won't be surprised when we get there," Isabel began. "For starters, there were only forty-six states back then. The population of Las Vegas was thirty. That's right. Just *thirty* people lived in Las Vegas!"

"Have you ever been to Vegas?" Luke asked. "It's *huge*. Anyway, back in those days, almost everybody was born at home, not in a hospital. And the average person lived to be about fifty years old. That's *it*."

"Oh man," David groaned. "My dad is fifty-two *now*."

"On the other hand," Isabel said, "you could mail a letter for two cents in 1912. A dozen eggs cost just fourteen cents."

"I would buy *everything*," David commented.

"Yeah, but the average adult only earned about two hundred to four hundred dollars a *year*," Luke explained.

"You've got to be kidding me," said Julia. "*I* make more than that from babysitting."

"The women's movement was very young in 1912," Isabel continued. "Women couldn't even vote yet. There was no civil rights movement. In a lot of places, black kids and white kids couldn't go to the same schools. And gay marriage? Forget about it. Gay people were, like, invisible back then."

"Oh, and by the way," Luke said, "there's a lot of stuff we have today that didn't exist in 1912. Like refrigerators, television, computers, traffic lights, zippers . . ."

"Really?" Julia asked. "No zippers? What did they use before they had zippers?"

"Buckles, laces, hooks—who knows?" Luke replied. "Anyway, we learned lots of other stuff, but you get the idea."

"Excellent work," Miss Z said, giving a quick round of applause. "It certainly was a different world back then. David, you're up next. What have you got for us?"

"Well, I checked out how people *talked* back in 1912," he said as he stood up with his notes. "Do you guys know what a beezer is?"

Everyone shook their heads. Even Miss Z didn't know.

"A beezer is your nose," David informed them. "Like, I'm going to punch you in the *beezer*. And if somebody in 1912 says they're *whacked*, it means they're tired. And if somebody says that something is *duck soup*, that means it's easy. Easy as duck soup."

"That's interesting," said Miss Z. "There was an old Marx Brothers movie called *Duck Soup*. I always wondered what that phrase meant."

"Lots of words we use these days were totally fresh in 1912," David continued, looking at his notes. "Stuff like rinky-dink, dingbat, doohickey, crackpot, loony bin. Man, rappers would have gone *crazy* with those words. I mean, if rapping had been invented yet. Oh, you know what word was coined that year? Vitamin! Vita means 'life' in Latin. There were no vitamins until 1912."

"I had no idea!" said Miss Z. "Nice work, David. Julia, your turn."

Julia jumped to her feet.

"Well, I decided to learn about the *fashions* of 1912," she said excitedly.

"What a shock," Luke mumbled under his breath.

Julia had put together a little scrapbook with photos she had found of fashions from 1912. She passed it around for everyone to see.

"Some of the richest and most famous people in the world were on the *Titanic*," she said. "The society ladies were all decked out, if you'll excuse the pun. They would change clothes several times a day so they had to have lots of outfits for every occasion. We're going to see them wearing gorgeous ankle-length evening gowns made from silk or chiffon or velvet. They'll be trimmed at the neck with lace and ribbons, glittering beads, sequin embroidery, maybe a mink stole around their necks—"

"If you ask me, they should have ditched all those fancy duds and brought life jackets with them," David remarked.

"Very funny," Julia said sarcastically.

"They didn't *have* to bring life jackets with them," Isabel told David. "There were life jackets in all the cabins on the *Titanic*."

"The ladies will all be wearing hats," Julia continued. "These enormous wide-brimmed hats decorated with flowers and ostrich feathers. And gloves. Elbow-length gloves. No proper lady would *ever* go out in public without gloves. And they'll be wearing silk stockings and dainty high-heeled shoes, or elegant leather boots with buttons . . ."

Julia was really getting into it. She loved everything having to do with fashion.

"And jewelry," she continued. "*Lots* of jewelry. Pearl earrings and necklaces, diamond rings—"

"What about the men?" interrupted Miss Z. "What did they wear?"

"Oh, the men pretty much all dressed the same, like they do today," Julia replied. "You know, pinstriped pants. Shiny black shoes. Overcoats. Gloves. Tuxedos.

They looked like a bunch of penguins."

"Okay, thank you, Julia," Miss Z said, reaching into her desk drawer. "You've all done a great job. Now it's time to get down to business. Here's a new TTT . . ."

She pulled out a small black box with two buttons on it and handed it to Isabel. The device was about the size of a cell phone.

TTT stands for Text Through Time. Miss Z had spent more than a billion dollars—a good chunk of her fortune—to create this gizmo that enables a person from one time period to communicate—by text—with a person in another time period. It's a breakthrough technology.

Someday, maybe in your lifetime, you'll be able to swap texts with your long lost relatives. Or you'll be able to send a text to *yourself* in the future—and receive a reply. It's hard to imagine, I know. It sounds like magic, but as the famous futurist Arthur Clarke once said, "Any sufficiently advanced technology is indistinguishable from magic."

In any case, the TTT will change the world. And Isabel was holding the only one in existence. She examined it carefully, turning it over in her hand.

"I want you to keep me informed every step of the way," Miss Z told the kids. "If something goes wrong, you need to text me *immediately* so I can get you out of there fast. Believe it or not, safety is more important to me than getting a picture of the *Titanic*. You are my responsibility. Your parents put their faith in me when they signed these permission forms."

Luke, Julia, David, and Isabel tried not to look at one another. They all knew that *none* of their parents had actually given permission for them to go on such a dangerous mission.

"If something happens to any of you, it will be my fault," Miss Z said seriously. "So whatever you do, don't lose the TTT this time."

"We didn't lose it the *last* time," Luke replied, a bit defensively. "After they locked us in jail at Gettysburg, the sheriff there smashed it."

"Well, don't let that happen again," Miss Z told him. "It will cost me almost a billion dollars to build another one. This is the only one of its kind. Now, you'll need a camera, of course . . ."

She opened her desk drawer again.

"Do we have to take such a *big* camera this time?" Luke asked. "That was our problem at Gettysburg. When the people in 1863 saw me pointing that thing at President Lincoln, they just freaked out. They had never seen a camera that looked like that. They thought I was going to shoot the president. I mean, shoot him with *bullets*."

"I hear you, and I'm listening," Miss Z said, pulling out a small box and handing it to Luke. "No more big cameras. This is a simple point-and-shoot. It fits in your pocket. Just turn it on, aim, press the button, and fire. Think you can handle that?"

"Oh yeah," Luke replied. "It will be, uh . . . duck soup."

"Good. Any questions?" Miss Z asked.

None of the kids had a question, but David clearly had something on his mind. He was looking down at the floor, refusing to make eye contact with anybody.

"David, is something bothering you?" Miss Z asked.

"Yeah," he finally replied. "I just don't see how you're going to drop us on a ship in the middle of the ocean."

"I was wondering that too," Luke said. "Isn't it sort of like landing a plane on a moving aircraft carrier? What if you miss? What if we end up in the water instead of on the *Titanic*?"

"Good question," Miss Z replied. "The answer is, don't worry about it. I know the exact coordinates of the *Titanic*."

"Huh?" the kids mumbled.

"The *what*?" asked Julia.

Miss Z rolled her eyes, the way grown-ups do when they can't believe kids don't know something that everybody is supposed to know.

"Didn't they teach you about latitude and longitude in school?" she asked the group.

"No."

"I think I was absent that day," Luke added.

Miss Z let out a sigh and mumbled something under her breath about kids today. Then she asked Luke to go over to the windowsill and get the globe that was sitting there. He brought it back and the Flashback Four leaned in to examine it.

"Look," Miss Z said. "The *Titanic* was built in Belfast. That's a city in Ireland. *Here*."

She pointed to Ireland on the globe and slid her finger slightly to the right.

"On April third, *Titanic* sailed to England. That's *here*. Some lucky people got off in England, and a bunch of not-so-lucky people got on board there. A week later, on Wednesday, April tenth, the *Titanic* set sail from Southampton, England, and stopped off in France to pick up some more passengers. *Here*. Then it headed across the Atlantic Ocean toward New York. *Here.* But of course, *Titanic* never reached New York. After three and a half days at sea, it hit the iceberg at *this* spot, about 370 miles southeast of Newfoundland. Right *here.*"

She traced a line with her finger across the Atlantic and stopped before she reached North America.

Location of *Titanic*

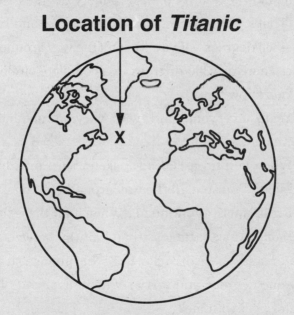

"I still don't see how you're going to land us on a moving ship," David said. "The ocean is so *big.*"

"I'm getting to that," Miss Z explained. "You kids

know what the equator is, right?"

"It's like, an imaginary line that goes around the middle of the Earth," Isabel replied, pointing to it on the globe.

"That's right," Miss Z said. "The equator is at zero degrees. Latitude is measured above and below the equator. So the North Pole is at ninety degrees north, and the South Pole is at ninety degrees south. See? That's 180 degrees from pole to pole, and twice that—360 degrees—if you went all the way around the globe. There are 360 degrees in a complete circle. Do you kids know that?"

"Yeah," everyone said, with varying amounts of assurance.

"When you do a 360 on a skateboard or a bike," Luke said, "you spin all the way around one time."

"Right," Miss Z continued. "When it hit the iceberg, the *Titanic* was a little less than halfway between the equator and the North Pole. To be precise, it was forty-one degrees and forty-six minutes north of the equator. Still with me?"

"I think so," Isabel said, even though she didn't quite understand why distance would be measured in degrees and minutes instead of miles or kilometers. But she decided to just go with the flow.

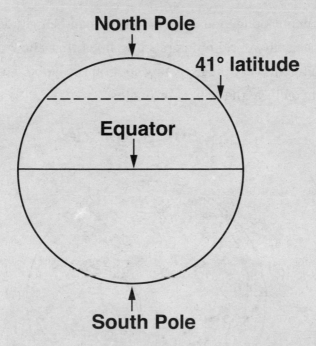

North Pole

41° latitude

Equator

South Pole

"Good," Miss Z said. "So that's the ship's *latitude*. Similarly, we can locate exactly where *Titanic* was east or west by its *longitude*."

"What's that?" David asked.

"There's no equator that cuts the Earth in half in this direction," Miss Z explained. "So back in 1851, it was agreed that zero degrees would cut through a point in Greenwich, England. The numbers get bigger from there, the same as they do with latitude. So if you head west from England, as the *Titanic* did, it struck the iceberg at exactly fifty degrees and fourteen minutes longitude. *Here.* So latitude and longitude are basically a grid of intersecting lines that allow us to pinpoint very precisely any spot on the globe. That is, if you have the right coordinates."

50° longitude

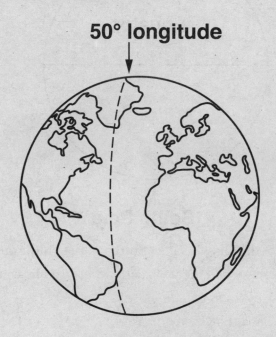

David still looked apprehensive about the whole thing.

"But how do you know the exact coordinates?" he asked. "What if your numbers are wrong?"

"I know they're right because the wireless had recently been invented, and the *Titanic* had one," Miss Z told him. "When it hit the iceberg, the ship stopped moving and the crew immediately began sending out distress signals. They broadcast their exact location, hoping that another ship would rescue them. Unfortunately, the nearest ship was four hours away, and by the time it got there, *Titanic* was gone. It sank at exactly 2:20 in the morning on April fifteenth."

"So you're going to send us to that exact spot and that exact time?" Julia asked.

"No, of course not," Miss Z said. "That would be foolish. I'm going to put you on the *Titanic* a couple of hours *before the collision*, so you'll have time to move around the ship and get your bearings before all the excitement begins."

"Wait a minute," Luke said. "A couple of hours before the collision, the *Titanic* wasn't *at* that exact location. Right? Because it was moving."

"Very good, Luke," Miss Z said. "Here's the thing. We know exactly how fast *Titanic* was moving that night. Twenty-four miles per hour. So I can extrapolate—do you know that word?—and figure out exactly where it was two hours before the collision."

"So it's sort of like in football when a quarterback throws a pass to his receiver, right?" Luke said. "He doesn't throw the ball where the receiver *is*. He throws

43

it where the receiver is going to *be*."

"Precisely!" said Miss Z. "I'm not going to throw you kids on the *Titanic* at the moment it sinks. You would drown! I'm going to throw you on the *Titanic* where it was two hours *before* it hit the iceberg."

"But not every football pass gets completed," David said, a worried look still on his face. "Sometimes the receiver drops the ball, or it gets intercepted. Sometimes the quarterback misses the target entirely."

"I promise you I won't miss the target," Miss Z assured David, putting a hand on the boy's shoulder.

"Okay," David said grudgingly.

"So, are you kids pumped?" asked Miss Z.

"I'm pumped!" said Luke.

"Totally pumped," said Julia.

"Me too," said Isabel.

Everyone looked at David, who *still* seemed apprehensive.

"What's the matter, David?" asked Miss Z.

He looked down silently again. It seemed like he might be on the verge of crying.

"You can tell us," Julia said, putting an arm around David.

"I'm afraid," he mumbled.

"Afraid of what?" Isabel asked. "Are you afraid

because of the way African Americans were treated back in those days?"

"No."

David didn't say anything for a long time.

"I . . . don't know how to swim, okay?" he finally admitted. "I'm afraid we're going to miss the ship and land in the water. And I'll drown. Okay? There, I said it."

The others went over to David and wrapped their arms around him. That only made his sobbing worse.

"It's okay," Isabel said.

"Dude," said Luke, "you *really* don't know how to swim? Seriously?"

"It wasn't a priority when I was little," David said, wiping his face with his sleeve. "So I never learned."

"Hey, I've got your back, man," Luke told him. "I took a lifesaving course a couple years ago. I swim like a fish. I won't let you drown."

David sniffled a bit and tried to pull himself together.

"David," Miss Z said, "you're in good hands. I know *exactly* when the collision took place. I know *exactly* where the *Titanic* sank. I know *exactly* how fast it was moving. I'm going to drop you right on that ship at *exactly* 9:40 p.m. on April fourteenth, 1912. Then I'm going to scoop you up and bring you back here at *exactly* 2:05 the next morning. That's fifteen minutes before the *Titanic* will sink."

"What if we need you to pick us up before that?" asked Isabel.

"Then I will," Miss Z assured her. "Just text me. As soon as you take the picture, send me a text and I'll get you out of there. I won't let anything happen to you. Everything is going to run smoothly. Can you trust me?"

"I guess so," David said.

"Here," Miss Z said, reaching into her pocket and pulling out a watch. "You're going to need this. I want you to wear it at all times, David."

"What's that?" Julia asked. "Some kind of new high-tech heart monitor?"

"It's à watch, you dope!" Luke told her, shaking his head in amazement.

"Hey, don't call me a dope!" Julia shot back. "You're the dope."

"It's an *analog* watch," Miss Z told Julia. "I hope you kids know how to read an analog watch. When the little hand is on the four and the big hand—"

"I know how to read an analog watch," David told her.

"Why can't we get a nice digital watch?" Julia asked. "They're much more accurate than analog."

"If the people in 1912 see a digital watch, they will totally freak out," Isabel told her.

"That's right," said Miss Z. "Don't take it off, don't break it, and whatever you do, don't put it under water. It's water-resistant, but it's not waterproof. Got it?"

"Got it," David said.

"Good," said Miss Z. "One last thing. We need to choose a meeting place where I can scoop you up after you take the photo. The *Titanic* is a *very* big ship, of course. We need to pick one spot we can all agree on."

"How about the main deck?" suggested Luke.

"The ship is huge," Miss Z said. "We have to pick a specific place on it."

"What about the king-of-the-world spot?" suggested Julia.

For a moment, all she got were blank looks.

"Remember the movie?" Julia asked. "You know that place at the front of the ship where Jack stood, and he yelled, 'I'm the king of the world'?"

"Oh yeah!" everyone replied.

"Perfect!" said Miss Z. "You need to be at that spot at exactly 2:05 a.m. I will bring you home from there."

"We'll be there," Isabel said, making a mental note of the time.

"I'm going to be honest with you," Miss Z said,

looking at the Flashback Four one at a time. "This is more dangerous than your trip to Gettysburg. We have no margin for error this time. If you mess up, it could be the end of you."

"And if *you* mess up, it could be the end of us too," said Luke.

"So let's not mess up."

GOING BACK

"YOU KIDS HAD BETTER GET DRESSED FOR THE trip," Miss Z said. "Boys first."

Mrs. Vader escorted Luke and David into a changing room next to her office, which Miss Z had thoughtfully built after the first Flashback Four trip. There were two outfits hanging in there, one for David (taller and thinner) and one for Luke (shorter and stockier). The girls waited excitedly for the boys to emerge from the changing room.

Five minutes passed.

"Boys!" hollered Miss Z. "Are you coming out?"

"No!" Luke and David shouted from behind the door.

"Come on," hollered Julia. "How bad could it be?"

"Bad!" the boys hollered back.

David came out of the changing room first, looking completely embarrassed. Both girls had to stifle their giggles when they saw what he was wearing—a dark wool suit, a white shirt with a stiffly starched collar, a bow tie, leather boots, and loose-fitting short pants that gathered just below the knee.

"What's with those pants?" asked Isabel.

"They're knickers," Miss Z and Mrs. Vader said together.

"I'm not wearing this monkey suit."

"But that's the way fashionable young men dressed in 1912," Miss Z told him. "Boys didn't wear long pants in those days until they were sixteen years old. You want to fit in, don't you?"

"No!" said David.

"You look *good*," Julia assured him, still trying not to laugh.

"Yeah, you look really cool, David!" Isabel said.

"Really?" he asked.

"No, I'm just trying to make you feel good."

"Gee, thanks," David said. "This thing doesn't even have a zipper on it. How can they have pants without zippers?"

"The zipper hadn't been invented in 1912," said Julia. "Remember?"

"At least I don't look as pathetic as Luke," David grumbled.

"Get out here, Luke!" shouted Miss Z.

"No!" he shouted back. "I'm *never* coming out."

"Oh, stop being a baby!" hollered Isabel.

Finally, the door to the changing room opened and Luke came out.

He was wearing a sailor suit.

Yes, he was dressed up like a sailor. Julia and Isabel just about fell off their chairs.

"You *gotta* be kidding me," said Julia, trying to regain her composure.

"Now I don't feel so bad," David said. "Compared to him, I look cool."

"I *knew* I shouldn't have come out," Luke said. "I look ridiculous."

"Don't be silly," said Miss Z. "*Lots* of boys wore sailor suits in 1912. Especially boys who were going on a transatlantic cruise. It was very trendy in those days. You'll be on the cutting edge of fashion."

"The cutting edge of nerditude," Luke whined.

"Oh, I almost forgot," Mrs. Vader said as she

rummaged through a box. "You boys need hats."

"What, so we can hide our faces?" asked David.

"A polite gentleman would *never* go outside without a hat on," Miss Z explained while Mrs. Vader took a few hats out of the box. "And he would *never* come inside without taking his hat *off*. That's just the way things were in those days."

Mrs. Vader gave Luke a sailor hat, of course. David picked out a plain dark wool hat and put it on his head backward.

"Ooh, look at me," he said, dancing around. "I have this cloth thing on my head. It makes me more polite."

"Oh stop it," Miss Z said, laughing. "It's just a hat. Be a good sport. Okay, girls, it's your turn."

The boys sat down. Julia and Isabel went to the fitting room, where Mrs. Vader had hung an outfit for each of them. They both came out a few minutes later, whirling around to show off their fancy dresses. Isabel was wearing a red flannel gown, and Julia had on a white cotton dress with puffed sleeves. Both girls were sporting oversized bonnets tied with large silk bows.

"You look fabulous," Mrs. Vader told the girls, applauding. "And you boys look *so* handsome!"

"I'll be the prettiest girl on the *Titanic*," Julia said,

striking a pose and giggling uncontrollably.

"Yeah," David said, rolling his eyes, "and one of the few who doesn't die."

"What if I have to run someplace?" asked Isabel. "I can't run in this dress."

"You won't have to run anywhere," David told her. "We'll take the photo and get out of there."

"Okay, let's get this thing over with," Luke said, putting the sailor hat on his head.

Miss Z turned to her computer and found the file she had created titled "FLASHBACK FOUR." Then she pointed a small remote control at the Board on the other side of the room. It buzzed gently as it turned on and flashed some quick messages to indicate it needed a little time to warm up.

The Board resembled an ordinary smartboard like the ones you may have in your school, but it was so much more. I could devote the next few pages to explain exactly how the Board works. I could talk about the speed of light and space-time and black holes and tunnels through the universe. But to be honest, time-travel is far too complicated for me to understand, and unless you're a physicist it would just sound like a lot of mumbo jumbo to you too.

Needless to say, the Board was packed full of

ridiculously expensive microprocessors, software, and advanced technology that is generations beyond anything you've seen or even heard of. People like Miss Z who have gobs of money can get hold of stuff that won't be available to the general public for many years.

The important thing to know is that the Board can send a person—or a group of people—to any moment and any spot on the globe if you plug in the exact time, latitude, and longitude. It works. Like magic. You'll have to take my word for it.

Luke, Isabel, Julia, and David stood up and went over to the Board, positioning themselves boy-girl-boy-girl. Miss Z motioned for them to move closer to the Board. Two feet was the perfect distance. Isabel checked to make sure she had the TTT. Luke patted his pocket to be certain the camera was in there.

"Okay, are you kids ready?" asked Miss Z, typing some commands on the keyboard.

"Ready as I'll ever be," Isabel replied.

"Promise you're not going to drop us in the ocean?" asked David.

"I promise," Miss Z told him. "Okay, this is it. You may want to close your eyes for the next minute or so. It's going to be pretty bright in here. Good luck.

Remember, stay together at all times. Work as a team. Keep in touch with me. Bring back that photo. And stay safe. That's what it's all about."

She tapped a few keys. There was a brief buzzing sound, and then the screen on the Board lit up in a blast of bright blue. After a few seconds, the blue split into five separate bands of different colors, and then they merged together to form one band of intense white light. It appeared to stretch out and away from the surface of the Board until it reached the kids. It was like the Board was sucking them in.

"The light!" Isabel said. "It's so *bright*. I can see it through my eyelids."

"You'll be able to open your eyes in a moment," Miss Z told her, "and it will be 1912."

An intense humming sound reverberated around the room, a low frequency rumbling like the purring of a gigantic cat.

"A few more seconds . . . ," said Miss Z.

Then, one by one, the kids started to flicker. It was almost imperceptible at first, but after a few seconds it became more obvious. It looked like a fluorescent light bulb that needed to be replaced.

It was happening. Luke, Isabel, David, and Julia were stepping out of one era and into another. At that point, it was too late to go back.

"This is it," Luke said. "Speak now, or forever hold your—"

And then they vanished.

CHAPTER

5

A SMALL CITY

SOMETHING WAS WRONG.

Something had gone *horribly* wrong. David knew it the instant he appeared in 1912. He wasn't on the deck of the *Titanic*. He had landed headfirst in the *water*.

"She missed!" he screamed, his mouth full of water as he struggled to keep his head above the surface. "I'm in the ocean! Help!"

Actually, David hadn't landed in the ocean. He had landed in a swimming pool. The swimming pool that happened to be in a large room on the deck of the *Titanic*.

"I can't swim!" he gagged, spitting out water. "I'm drowning! Somebody help me!"

Luke, Julia, and Isabel had landed right next to the

pool, just inches from the edge. Luke grabbed both girls by the elbows and pulled them back just before they would have fallen in too. Fortunately, no other passengers were in the pool room at the time to witness this strange event.

"I've got you, dude!" Luke shouted to David. Thinking fast, he took the camera out of his pocket and handed it to Isabel to hold. Then he dove into the pool.

The water was only about six feet deep, and David could have simply stood on his tiptoes to keep his head above the surface. But he didn't know that. He flailed his arms around wildly in a desperate attempt to avoid going under for a second time.

Luke swam over, wrapped one arm firmly around David's chest, and pulled him to the side of the pool.

"You're okay!" Luke whispered in his friend's ear. "I've got you, man. Everything's gonna be okay!"

David managed to grab a metal bar and hoist himself out of the water. He lay on the blue and white tiles at the edge, spitting, sputtering, and heaving.

"Miss Z didn't tell us . . . there was a swimming pool," he groaned.

Luke climbed out of the pool, chuckling a little to himself. He grabbed a towel that said RMS TITANIC on it and wiped his face with it. He tossed another one to David.

"I almost died!" David shouted. "It's not funny!"

"Not to you, maybe," Luke said. The girls tried to hide their smiles behind their hands. That's when Isabel noticed David's wrist.

"The watch!" she said, grabbing David's arm. "The second hand isn't moving. Miss Z told us not to get it wet, and now it's ruined. She's going to be mad."

"It's *her* fault," Julia said. "She's the one who dumped David in the pool. She can't blame us this time."

"It doesn't matter whose fault it is," Luke said. "How will we know when it's five minutes after two? That's when Miss Z said for us to be at the meeting spot so she can bring us back home."

"We better check in with her," Isabel said as she pulled out the TTT. "I'm just glad *I* didn't fall in the pool. This would be ruined too."

Isabel turned on the TTT and texted this message . . .

LANDED SAFELY ON TITANIC

A few seconds later, a response came back from Miss Z . . .

GREAT! ANY PROBLEMS?

DAVID LANDED IN SWIMMING POOL, Isabel texted. THE WATCH IS BUSTED.

OKAY, Miss Z texted back. NO WORRIES. JUST ASK SOMEBODY WHAT TIME IT IS.

Of course. Lots of passengers would be wearing watches. Simple problem, simple solution. A *bigger* problem was that Luke's and David's clothes were now soaking wet. And these were the only clothes they had.

Luke looked around, as if a rack of men's clothes would be conveniently placed next to the swimming pool. It wasn't, of course. But there was a men's locker room in the corner.

There were no clothes in there either, but hanging from hooks on the wall were several fancy navy blue bathrobes with the words RMS TITANIC embroidered on the backs in red. They were there for the passengers to take.

"Nice!" David said. "And these will make cool souvenirs to bring home. They're a lot cooler than those lame clothes Miss Z gave us."

"You're telling me," Luke said, pulling off his sailor suit.

The boys put on the bathrobes and couldn't resist strutting a little as they came out of the locker room.

"Check out our new duds," David told the girls.

"Now we look *cool*," said Luke.

"You've *got* to be kidding me," Julia said. "Bathrobes? Really?"

"Is *that* all you're wearing?" asked Isabel.

"We kept our underwear on," Luke explained. "What, do you have a better idea?"

"Boxers or briefs?" asked Julia.

"None of your business," David replied.

Neither of the girls could come up with a better idea, so the Flashback Four left the swimming pool and walked out on the main deck. The smell of fresh paint was in the air. That's how new the *Titanic* was.

"This is it," Luke said, marveling at the whole experience. "We're on the *Titanic*."

The sun had already set, and the sky was dark. They estimated that it was past ten o'clock, because Miss Z had said they would arrive at 9:40. It wasn't a windy night, but it was cold enough to see your breath when you exhaled. Luke pulled his bathrobe tightly around him.

"Can you imagine how cold that water is?" Julia asked as she leaned over the railing and looked down. It was a *long* way down.

"Close to freezing," Isabel replied. "I looked it up back home. That's why so many people are going to die tonight. They're not going to drown. They're going to freeze to death."

The thought of people dying made everyone stop

for a moment. To the Flashback Four, the tragedy of the *Titanic* was no longer some fuzzy legend that took place more than a century ago. They weren't reading about it in a book or watching a Hollywood movie. It was immediate, and it was unfolding before their eyes.

Reminded of their mission, the team set out to get their bearings on the ship. Their first priority was to find the spot where they would meet so they could be scooped up off the deck before *Titanic* sank—the I'm-the-king-of-the-world spot.

The first thing you notice on a huge vessel is that it doesn't even feel like you're on a boat. It's just so big. There were nine decks on the *Titanic*, and the whole ship was about the height of an eleven-story build-ing. When it rocked up and down or back and forth, the passengers could barely sense any movement. At the time, *Titanic* was the largest human-made moving object in the world. It was more like a small city that happened to be floating in the ocean.

And what a city it was! *Titanic* had its own hospi-tal, a library, two barber shops, squash courts, and a darkroom for developing pictures. The crew pub-lished a daily newspaper called *Atlantic Daily Bulletin*. There were five pianos on board and four elevators.

Besides the swimming pool there was a state-of-the-art (for its time) gym, and a Turkish steam bath that was decorated like a room in a sultan's palace. The layout of the ship was so complicated that when they got on board, all the passengers were given a guide book to help them find their way around.

There were two elegant restaurants—the Café Parisien and the À la Carte. In order to feed over two thousand people, the *Titanic* was stocked with a hundred thousand pounds of beef, thirty thousand eggs, and fifty tons of potatoes.

Hidden out of sight, in the bowels of the ship, were 159 furnaces and twenty-nine boilers that generated the steam to power the engines, each one the size of a large room. *Titanic* burned 650 tons of coal a day.

The only thing missing from *Titanic* was enough lifeboats to hold all those passengers and crew members after the whole thing went underwater.

Many of the passengers had retired to their staterooms for the night, but there were some scattered loners and lovers out for a late stroll. The women were dressed exactly the way Julia had predicted they would be, in fancy dresses, enormous hats, and lots of jewelry.

"The ladies are *so* beautiful!" Julia marveled.

"That one by the rail looks like she's wearing the drapes," cracked David.

Waiters were hustling around serving people coffee and tea. Luke boldly walked up to one of them.

"Excuse me, my good man," he said. "Can you tell me what time it is?"

"Certainly," the waiter replied, pulling out one of those old-timey watches attached to a chain in his pocket. "It's ten minutes after ten o'clock. Past bedtime for you young folks, I'd say. Do your parents know where you are?"

"Oh, I think this is going to be a late night," Luke said.

Once the waiter was out of earshot, David pulled Luke aside.

"We're just observers, remember?" he said sternly. "We're not allowed to do *anything* that might change history."

"What history could I change?" Luke replied. "I'm just stating facts. We're going to hit the iceberg at 11:40. That's about an hour and a half from now. It's going to be a late night for *everybody* on this ship tonight."

Standing at the rail and looking down at the water, Isabel seemed lost in thought. Both of the boys went over to see if she was okay.

"This is like a miniature world," she said. "All the rich people are up here on the top deck eating, relaxing, and laughing in their fancy clothes. The poor people who scraped together enough money to come to America must be in the decks below us. And then at the bottom there must be even poorer people—the laborers who shovel coal into the furnaces. It must take *hundreds* of people working night and day to keep a ship like this moving forward."

David rolled his eyes.

"It's just a *boat*," he said. "You don't need to get all sentimental about it."

"Yeah," Luke added, "there are rich people and

poor people here. Just like anyplace else."

"I guess you're right," Isabel sighed. "But a whole lot of them aren't going to be alive in a few hours."

"That can't be our problem," Luke told her. "We have a job to do. Come on, let's go find the meeting spot."

The three of them wheeled around to see . . . nobody.

"Where's Julia?" all three said at once.

DECISIONS

JULIA HAD DISAPPEARED. NOT IN THE *POOF!* SENSE of the word. She just wasn't there anymore.

"She was here a minute ago," David said, quickly looking up and down the deck.

"Oh no!" Isabel said. "Maybe she fell overboard! Or do you think maybe she was kidnapped?"

"She wasn't kidnapped," Luke said, rolling his eyes. "Who would kidnap her? She must have run away, *again*. Remember what happened at Gettysburg?"

Of course they did. How could they forget? Soon after they had arrived in Gettysburg, Julia had vanished. The other members of the Flashback Four had tracked her down to the room where Abraham Lincoln was staying that night. This was where Lincoln would finish writing the Gettysburg Address. Julia knew that there were only five existing copies of the speech in Lincoln's handwriting. Her idea was to grab one so she could make a fortune selling it after she got home.

Not that Julia needed money, of course. She just enjoyed the thrill of getting it.

"We've got to find her," Isabel said urgently.

At that moment, the TTT buzzed in her pocket.

"Ignore it!" David said, but Isabel dutifully checked the message from Miss Z . . .

DID YOU MAKE IT TO THE MEETING PLACE?

"Forget about that!" Luke told Isabel. "We don't have time to chat with her now! Julia's getting away!"

But Isabel had been brought up to respect her elders. It would be wrong to ignore Miss Z's text. She typed . . .

JULIA IS MISSING

The response came back almost instantly.

WHAT? WHERE IS SHE?

"If we knew where she was, she wouldn't be missing," David pointed out.

DON'T KNOW, Isabel typed.

GO FIND HER! Miss Z replied.

"She must have ducked inside one of the

staterooms," David said, snapping into action. "I'll look down this way. Isabel, you go that way. Luke, check over there. Let's meet back here in ten minutes whether we find her or not. We've got to stay together."

"Right!" shouted Isabel and Luke.

Each of the three ran off in a different direction to search for Julia. The *Titanic* was enormous, of course, but Julia had only been gone for a few seconds. She couldn't be very far away.

The two boys headed toward the bow and stern (that's the front and back of a ship, to you landlubbers), and Isabel ducked down the nearest hallway.

There were a bunch of stateroom doors down the twisting hallway, and Isabel heard footsteps ahead of her. She followed them, trying to be as quiet as possible as she ran. The stateroom doors were all closed. Some of them had small signs with names on them. MR. AND MRS. STRAUS. THE MARTIN BROTHERS. The footsteps always seemed to be a few turns ahead of her. And then they stopped. A door clicked shut.

"Julia!" Isabel half whispered and half shouted. "Julia, where are you?"

There was no answer. Isabel looked up and down the row of stateroom doors, hoping that one of them would open again. None of them did, so she tried turning doorknobs. The first five were locked. The next one turned. Isabel pushed open the door quietly.

Julia was standing there, hunched over a chest of drawers.

"Julia!"

Julia gasped, startled. She had something in her hand, and quickly shoved it into a drawer before turning around.

"Isabel! What are you doing here?" she whispered. "You scared me to death!"

"What are *you* doing here?" Isabel asked. "You know we're supposed to stay together as a group. What's in that drawer?"

"Nothing."

"What is it?" Isabel insisted.

Julia sighed. She had the mind of a master thief but lacked the technique.

"Remember that blue diamond necklace that Rose had in the *Titanic* movie?" she asked Isabel. "It was called the Heart of the Ocean."

"That was just a movie," Isabel told her. "The necklace never existed in the real world."

"I know," Julia explained as she turned around to open the drawer, "but there were lots of diamonds and precious objects that were lost on the *Titanic*. And this is the most valuable one of them all."

She pulled out a leather-bound book titled *Rubai-yat of Omar Khayyam* and handed it to Isabel. There was a drawing of three golden peacocks on the cover. They were surrounded by gold embroidery and colorful jewels.

"It's *beautiful*," Isabel admitted, opening the book carefully.

"And it's priceless," Julia whispered. "It's a book of poems by Omar Khayyam. He was a Persian poet and mathematician in the eleventh century. This is a rare English translation. It was made with over a thousand rubies and emeralds."

Isabel read the first line on the first page . . .

*"AWAKE! For Morning in the Bowl of Night
Has flung the Stone that puts the Stars to
Flight . . ."*

"A few weeks before the *Titanic* sailed from England, the book was sold at an auction there," Julia explained. "An American antique book collector bought it, so the auction house is shipping it to him in New York."

"How do you know all this?" Isabel asked, handing

the book back to Julia. "And how did you know where to find it?"

"How does anybody know about anything?" Julia replied. "I Googled it."

"Julia, you could get in big trouble! This is very wrong."

"*Please* don't tell the boys," Julia begged. "They wouldn't understand. Can't we just keep this between you and me? This book must be worth *millions*. I'll split the money with you."

"Put it *back*," said a voice behind them. Both girls jumped and gasped. Julia nearly dropped the book.

It was Luke and David. Luke took the book from Julia's hand.

"This doesn't belong to you," he said.

"We're not supposed to change history," said David.

"Oh, come on!" Julia protested. "If we leave it here, it's going to go down with the ship, you know. It will be lost forever, and nobody will get it. But if I take it, we can prevent that from happening. What harm is there if I take it?"

"It's stealing," Isabel told her. "Stealing is wrong."

"And it's stealing from people who are going to *die*," Luke said, putting the book back inside the drawer carefully. "Don't you have any conscience?

Why do you do these things?"

Julia hung her head.

"I couldn't resist," she admitted. "I just thought I could grab it and go. Nobody would ever know."

"*We* would know," David told her. "And I for one don't want to keep your secrets."

"If you hadn't followed me here," Julia told him, "you wouldn't have known. I could have just taken the book and it would be done. Everybody would be happy."

Luke stopped before opening the stateroom door to leave.

"Don't mess this up for us!" he said, getting right in Julia's face. "We didn't come here to steal stuff. We came here to take a picture and get away before the ship sinks. So come on. Let's get out of here."

"I'm sorry," Julia said as they left the stateroom and closed the door behind them. "I'm *really* sorry."

FOUND HER! Isabel texted to Miss Z as soon as they got back out to the main deck. **NO WORRIES.** She didn't go into further detail.

All of us encounter moral decisions in life. Sometimes they're easy decisions. Stealing is almost always wrong. Lying is almost always wrong. Helping little old ladies cross the street is almost always right.

But sometimes, decisions like these aren't so simple. Robin Hood could argue that stealing from the rich to give to the poor could be the right thing to do. You could argue that lying to your aunt and telling her you love the hideous sweater she gave you for your birthday is the right thing to do. And helping a little old lady is probably wrong if she's robbing a bank as soon as she crosses the street.

The Flashback Four had made a moral decision not to take the jewel-encrusted *Rubaiyat of Omar Khayyam*. And now they were going to face a more difficult decision.

It was past ten thirty. In about an hour, the *Titanic* would hit the iceberg. Other than Julia, Isabel, David and Luke, nobody on board had a clue. As the kids made their way toward their meeting place at the bow of the ship, there were a lot more passengers outside enjoying a late-night stroll on deck. Some guys in military uniforms were horsing around with each other. A young couple was kissing. An elderly couple walked arm in arm. A crew member was swabbing the deck with a mop.

"Good evening," a man said as he passed, tipping his hat.

"Lovely night, eh?" said a woman with a British

accent. "A bit nippy, but just lovely."

Isabel went to the rail to look out at the water.

"I have a bad feeling inside," she said.

"Me too," David agreed. "I wonder which of these people out here are going to live and which ones are going to die."

"Most of the men are going to die," Luke said. "I know that for sure. The lifeboats are going to be filled with the women and children first. And a lot of the boats won't even be filled."

"Only about seven hundred people are going to survive," said Julia. "Most of the passengers are going to die. Especially the ones in third class. I looked it up."

They walked along slowly, passing a woman who was pushing a cute baby girl in a carriage. Maybe that baby would be a survivor. Maybe not.

"Do you think it's wrong for us to take a picture of the ship as it's sinking?" Isabel wondered out loud.

"What do you mean?" asked Julia. "How can taking a picture be wrong?"

"Isn't it sort of like witnessing a traffic accident, taking a few pictures, and then just driving away without helping?" Isabel asked. "It just feels wrong to me."

"It *is* kinda morbid," David said.

"Are you saying we should *do* something about it?"

Luke asked. "You know we're here to *record* history, not to change it."

"I know," Isabel said. "But think of it! We could save the lives of fifteen hundred innocent people! That baby in the carriage we just passed may die tonight. She'll never have the chance to live a life, go to school, have a career, and have kids of her own someday. For all we know, she could grow up to be the next Einstein."

"Or she could grow up to be the next Hitler," Julia said. "What could we do about it, anyway?"

"Simple," Luke replied. "We could alert the captain. If he knew the ship was going to hit an iceberg, he could steer around it. No collision. No tragedy."

"No news," added Julia. "No Hollywood movie."

"And no photo," David noted. "What would Miss Z say if she zapped us back to Boston and it turned out that the *Titanic* never sank at all?"

"That would be weird," Luke said. "She wouldn't even know why she sent us here in the first place."

"She might say we did the right thing," Isabel said. "She's not a cold-hearted person. I say let's vote on it. All in favor of alerting the captain, raise your hand."

Isabel put her hand up immediately. David put his hand up slowly, as if he wasn't sure. Julia saw the two hands up and decided to put hers up too. Finally, Luke reluctantly put his hand up.

"I guess I'm in," he said.

It was unanimous. The Flashback Four decided to warn the captain that the ship was going to hit an iceberg at exactly 11:40 p.m., so he would be able to steer around it. Now all they needed to do was find the captain.

"We need to go to the bridge," David said.

"The bridge? What's that?" asked Julia.

"How should I know?" said David. "But in movies, the captain of a ship is always on the bridge."

There was nothing in sight that looked even remotely like a bridge. But a steward rushed by wearing a crisp navy blue uniform. The words WHITE STAR LINE were on the brim of his hat. The Flashback Four ran over to stop him.

"Excuse me," David said. "We need to speak to the captain."

"The captain is asleep," the steward replied brusquely, glancing at his watch. "He retires every night at ten thirty with strict orders to not be disturbed unless there is an emergency."

"This *is* an emergency!" Isabel told him. "The ship is going to sink!"

The steward looked at her with disdain, rolling his eyes.

"Look, I have work to do," he said. "You kids better run along to bed or I'll tell your mommies."

With that, he hurried away.

"That guy was just a flunkie," Luke said. "We gotta find somebody more important, somebody who can get us to the captain."

In Isabel's pocket, the TTT buzzed.

DID YOU GET TO THE MEETING SPOT? it said on the screen. **WHAT'S TAKING SO LONG?**

ON OUR WAY, Isabel texted back. **IT'S A BIG SHIP!**

They passed some more passengers at the rail, and then Julia spotted a cluster of well-dressed men standing in the middle of the deck. They were all smoking cigars and clinking their glasses as they drank and

laughed. Two of them were wearing top hats.

One of the men seemed to be the center of atten-tion. He was thin, fiftyish, with a high forehead and a bushy mustache. He was wearing an expensive-look-ing pinstriped suit and he carried a walking stick even though it didn't look like he had any disability. The other men were gathered around him as he regaled them with a story. Julia strained to catch a snippet of the conversation.

"Wait, I think I know who that guy is!" she whis-pered to Isabel, David, and Luke.

"Which one?" Isabel asked.

"The guy with the big mustache. I think he's John Jacob Astor IV!"

"Never heard of him," David said.

"He's one of the richest men in the world," Julia told them. "He's got eighteen cars. He's worth some-thing like eighty million dollars. That's eighty million dollars in *1912*! He would be worth *billions* in our time."

"How do you know all this stuff?" Luke asked. "And how would you know what this Astor guy looks like?"

"How does anybody know anything? I Googled it!" Julia replied. "John Jacob Astor is the most famous person who died on the *Titanic*. If we can get to him, I bet we can get to the captain. Contacts are everything, you know."

"I wouldn't know how to talk to a guy like that," Luke said. "I don't know any rich people."

"Don't look at me," David said. "He's not going to take the advice of a black kid."

Julia looked at Isabel, who just shrugged.

"Okay, *I'll* do it," Julia finally said.

She took a deep breath, and marched over to the group of men.

"Excuse me, Mr. Astor?" she said, a big smile on her face.

The men turned to face Julia. They seemed shocked and somewhat amused that a girl so young would have the audacity to break into their conversation.

"May I help you, young lady?" asked Astor, bending over to pat Julia on the head.

"My name is Julia Brennan," she said, extending her hand, "and these are my friends Isabel, David, and Luke."

The others reluctantly stepped forward. Astor shook Julia's hand.

"It is my pleasure to meet you," Astor said. "And what can I do for you this fine evening?"

"I have some bad news, unfortunately," Julia said nervously. "In about an hour, the ship is going to hit an iceberg, and it's going to sink. The ship, I mean. Not the iceberg. The iceberg isn't going to sink."

"Is that so?" John Jacob Astor replied, amused.

"Yes," Julia continued. "The captain is asleep. It's very important that someone alert him so he can steer around it. Around the iceberg, that is."

John Jacob Astor and his cronies stared at Julia for a few seconds. Then, as a group, they broke up laughing. Several of them doubled over. It was as if they had just heard the funniest joke in the world.

"She's telling the truth," Isabel said, stepping forward. "This ship is going to sink. Many people are going to die. *You're* going to die, Mr. Astor."

"Well, I guess we're *all* going to die at some point," Astor said, pulling out a handkerchief to wipe his eyes. "Young women today! One never knows what they will come up with next. Am I right, fellows?"

Astor's cronies nodded their heads and laughed.

"I haven't had a howl like that in a long time," one of the men said.

"No, I *mean* it!" Julia said, with urgency in her voice. "In a few hours, this ship will be at the bottom of the ocean, and all of you will be down there with it. There aren't enough lifeboats, and they're going to fill them with the women and children first."

John Jacob Astor no longer seemed amused.

"And how, may I ask, do you know all this, young lady?" he asked.

Julia stopped herself just before she would have told him to Google it. She turned to the other members of the Flashback Four for help. Luke stepped forward.

"It doesn't matter how we know it, Mr. Astor," he said. "We just *do*. You've got to wake up the captain right away and let him know."

"Young man," said Astor, who didn't like *anybody* telling him what to do, much less a kid, "for centuries, man has sailed the seas, building bigger and stronger and safer vessels. Look around you. This ship is the pinnacle of what we have been able to achieve with our advanced technology. *Titanic* is unsinkable. Everyone knows that."

One of Astor's top-hatted cronies put a hand on Luke's shoulder. "Civilization is always improving itself," he said. "You will learn that as you grow up, young man. Progress marches on. This is a most wonderful time to be alive. For the first time in history, man can control nature. Why, those bicycle mechanics in North Carolina even figured out how to build a flying machine. Imagine that! A machine that can fly and even carry a passenger. Mark my words, someday we will be *flying* across this ocean. We find a problem and we use our brains to solve it. That's the American way! Right, fellows?"

"Right," said Astor. "So leave the important matters to us. Why don't you kids go play with your toys or something?"

Astor and his friends started to turn away, but Julia and Luke were not about to give up. Convincing Astor could very possibly be their only chance to save the ship. Luke grabbed the millionaire's elbow to turn him around.

"Look," he said. "I know you're really rich and famous. But that's not going to save you tonight. We know what we're talking about. I can't tell you how I know, but I know. You can save fifteen hundred lives, including your own. But you've got to help us. There isn't much time."

"Take your hand off me, young man!" Astor shot back, glaring. "Just who do you think you are?"

Several of Astor's cronies grabbed Luke and pulled him away, roughing him up a bit in the process. Julia and Isabel tried to stop them.

"Hey, leave him alone!" David said. "You can't do that!"

"We came from the twenty-first century!" Julia

shouted as the men pushed her away. "We know what's going to happen tonight."

"You children are disturbing the other passengers!" Astor yelled. "We booked passage on this ship to relax, not to listen to your insane rantings! Stop this right now, or I will call for my bodyguards!"

"This ship is going to hit an iceberg!" hollered Isabel. "You should be getting the lifeboats ready. Get on your lifejackets!"

At that moment, three burly men came running over and grabbed the Flashback Four.

SECOND THOUGHTS

"GET YOUR FILTHY HANDS OFF ME!" JULIA shrieked as one of John Jacob Astor's bodyguards wrapped his hairy arm around her neck.

"Oh, she's a feisty one," he said, sneering. He clapped one hand over Julia's mouth to keep her quiet, and she tried to bite it.

"Nobody talks that way to Mr. Astor!" shouted the thug who had grabbed Isabel and Luke. The third one had David in a headlock as the boy punched and kicked and struggled to get free.

"Get them out of here, fellows," said Mr. Astor. "We were having such a pleasant evening until these hooligans showed up."

"This is a free country!" Luke yelled, desperately

trying to break away. "I know my rights. You can't do this to us."

"This is *no* country," Astor replied. "We are in international waters, young man. I can do whatever I want."

"You don't understand!" Isabel shouted at Astor as the bodyguards dragged the Flashback Four away. "We're trying to save you! The ship is going to hit an iceberg! It's going down!"

"We came from the future," Julia added, trying to be helpful. "We know everything that's going to happen tonight!"

John Jacob Astor and his friends shook their heads, chuckling among themselves.

"Crazy kids," one of them muttered as he lit another cigar.

"In my day, children knew how to behave themselves," said his friend with a top hat. "Not anymore."

"You know what they say," John Jacob Astor told the group. "Children are to be seen and not heard. And sometimes, they shouldn't even be seen!"

His cronies laughed uproariously, as they did whenever Astor said just about anything that was even mildly funny.

Meanwhile, the Flashback Four were taken away roughly, dragged through a series of twisting corridors, and brought down several flights of stairs until they reached a lower deck of the ship that had plain, dark walls, bare floors, and no fancy staterooms. There was nothing elegant about this part of the *Titanic*. It was used to store luggage and oversized items that people had paid to ship to America.

"Stop it! You're hurting me!" Julia shouted as one of Astor's bodyguards pushed her against a door and took a key out of his pocket.

"You keep your mouth shut before I shut it up for you!" the thug replied.

Keeping one hand on Julia's arm, he used his other hand to open the door. All four kids were shoved into the room.

"This ought to hold you for a while," one of the bodyguards said. "See you in New York!"

"Wait! Stop!" David shouted just before the door slammed shut.

They could hear the key click inside the lock from the other side of the door. David tried to turn the doorknob. It wouldn't budge. They were locked in.

Luke had landed on the floor, his chest heaving. His leg was scratched, but more than that his pride was wounded. Luke was a big guy. He had been in a few playground fights, and he knew how to handle himself. But in the end, he was just a boy. John Jacob Astor's thugs had simply overpowered him.

It was a bare-bones room. There was a wooden bed with no mattress in the corner and pretty much nothing else. A light bulb hanging from a wire on the ceiling provided the only light. It looked like a prison cell.

For a few long moments, none of the Flashback Four said anything. They just sat on the floor, trying not to make eye contact with each other.

"I *told* you coming here was a bad idea," Isabel finally said, breaking the silence. "You wouldn't listen to me."

"You were right," agreed David. "We never should have taken on this mission. It was too dangerous. Something was bound to go wrong."

"I thought we'd just be able to take the picture and leave," Luke said. "Nobody could have predicted *this* was going to happen."

"Why not?" asked Isabel. "We tell some rich guy the ship is going to sink, and of *course* he's going to react negatively. Did you think he was going to listen to *us*?"

"How *else* were we going to get the point across?" asked Julia. "I didn't see any of *you* coming up with a better idea."

"No idea is better than a bad idea," David muttered.

"Stop arguing!" Luke shouted. "It doesn't matter anymore. It's in the past. We need to live in the present."

The present meaning 1912. Luke was right, of course. Arguing over what caused a bad situation is usually a waste of time. Nobody likes to admit they're wrong, and nobody likes to be criticized.

"That Astor guy is a jerk," Isabel said softly. "And he must have thought we were nuts."

"Where do you think we are?" Luke asked, looking around the dingy room.

"All I know is, we were dragged down three flights of stairs to get here," David said. "I counted. We're below the main deck."

"What are we going to do *now*?" Julia asked.

"Maybe we should send a text to Miss Z," suggested Isabel.

"Why? What's she gonna do?" asked Luke. "She can't help us in here. She's just going to say we messed up again."

As if on cue, the TTT buzzed in Isabel's pocket.

DID YOU GET TO THE MEETING PLACE YET? the screen read.

"What should I tell her?" Isabel whispered, as if Miss Z could hear her.

"Don't tell her what happened," Julia advised.

"She'll be angry and blame us. Just lie. Tell her everything is fine."

Isabel hesitated before responding to Miss Z's text. She didn't like to lie. And like David, she wasn't very good at it. Unlike Julia, she hadn't had much practice.

WE R THERE, Isabel typed, grimacing the whole time.

GREAT, Miss Z texted back immediately. I WILL PICK YOU UP FROM THAT SPOT AT 2:05 AM.

David looked at his watch and then remembered that it had stopped when he fell in the swimming pool. There was no way to know the exact time.

"It must be after eleven o'clock by now," Luke said. "If we don't get out of here and get to the meeting spot by 2:05, we won't be able to get back home."

"And if that happens, we'll have to start life all over again in 1912," David said.

"That's not necessarily a bad thing," Julia told him. "If we live the rest of our lives starting in 1912, we'll know lots of stuff that nobody else knows. Think about it. We'll be able to predict who will win the presidential elections. We'll know which companies, like McDonald's and Coca-Cola, are going to become huge. We could make a fortune on the stock market!"

"You have to have *money* to invest in the stock market," said Luke.

"That may be great for *you* guys, but what about me?" asked David. "The civil rights movement isn't going to start for a *long* time. In case you didn't know, they didn't treat black folks so great in the 1920s and 1930s. I don't want to start life all over again. I like our time better."

"Are you guys *crazy*?" Isabel asked. "I can't believe you're talking about starting over. None of us is going to start life all over again in 1912! This is going to be the *end* of our lives! If we don't get out of here, we're all going to *die* tonight! This will be the end of us."

Luke stood up.

"Isabel's right," he said. "Let's put our heads together and figure a way out of this. We're locked in a room. It's three floors below the main deck. We may even be below the waterline."

"That's where the iceberg is going to tear open the ship," Isabel said. "And that's where the water is going to come in first. We're sunk. Literally."

"So we've got to find a way out of this room, and fast," Luke said.

The door was locked. There was no window or porthole. Luke pushed his shoulder against the door to test it, but it was obvious that he wasn't strong enough. He looked over at the bed in the corner.

"Give me a hand with this," he told David, picking up one side of the bed.

"What are you doing?" asked Julia.

"We're going to ram the bed against the door and try to bust it down," Luke explained.

"Isn't that dangerous?" asked Isabel.

"Drowning is dangerous too," David told her.

He picked up the other side of the bed. It was heavy, and the two boys struggled to lift it.

Luke angled the bed so that one of its corners was pointed directly at the door, about three feet away.

"Okay," Luke said. "On the count of three, let's give it all we've got. Ready? One . . . two . . . three."

They rammed the corner of the bed against the metal door. It made a loud noise, but that was about it. They put the bed down to rest their shoulders.

"I think we need to swing it a little," David told Luke. "We need to get more momentum."

"Yeah, let's try it again," Luke said, picking up his side of the bed as David picked up the other side. Together they rocked the bed back and forth a few times, like it was a baby.

"One . . . two . . . three!"

Bang!

Nothing. The bed made a big noise but only a small

dent when it hit the door.

"I think you guys need a little help," Isabel said, jumping up to take a corner of the bed. Julia got up and took a corner as well. Luke and David slid over so that each of the Flashback Four was holding up one corner of the bed. With four people, it felt a lot lighter. The weight of it was distributed evenly.

"I think the door might have buckled a little that last time," David said. "One more time should do it."

"Okay, are you guys ready?" Luke asked.

"Yeah!"

They swung the bed back and forth a few times to build up momentum.

"One . . . two . . . *three*!" everybody shouted.

On three, they heaved the corner of the bed against the door as hard as they could.

BAM!

I'd like to be able to tell you that the door swung open and the Flashback Four dashed into the hallway to freedom. Unfortunately that's not what happened.

What happened was that the bed broke.

The force of the wood slamming into the metal door caused the sides of the bed to come apart in their hands as the Flashback Four fell all over themselves on the floor. The door didn't move an inch.

"Okay!" David said. "That was a bad idea. Anybody have any *other* ideas?"

"We're going to get in trouble!" Isabel said. "Look at this bed! It's in pieces."

"You think we're not *already* in trouble?" David asked. "We're locked in a room inside the *Titanic. That's* trouble!"

"Don't worry about the bed," Luke said. "It's going to end up at the bottom of the Atlantic Ocean anyway. With *us*."

"Well *I've* got a better idea," Julia said.

She picked up one of the planks of wood that used to make up one side of the bed. Then she slammed it, like a giant baseball bat, against the door. It made a loud slapping noise.

"Did anybody out there hear that?" she shouted at the top of her lungs. "We're locked up in here!"

"That's not a bad idea," Luke said, picking up one of the other planks. He swung it against the door, and Julia waited until he was finished before taking a second swing.

David and Isabel each picked up a piece of wood, and soon all four kids were slamming planks against the door, the ceiling, the walls, anything that would make noise and hopefully attract some attention.

"Help!" they screamed. "Let us out! Is anybody out there? Open the door!"

After a few minutes of this frantic activity with no success, Julia, Isabel, David, and Luke were exhausted. One by one they sat back on the floor, panting and sweating. For a long time, they just sat there, trying to think of what to do next.

Somewhere in the distance, a bell clanged three times.

"It's hopeless," David said. "We're stuck in here. We're going to die in this room, you know. There's nothing we can do about it."

Julia was the first one to begin sobbing. That set off a chain reaction, and before long all four of the Flashback Four were in tears.

"I'm too young to die," Julia sniffled.

Before anybody could respond to that, there was a sound that came from outside the room. It was barely audible, but distinct, and different.

"Did you hear that noise?" Isabel asked, no longer crying.

"Hear what?" Luke said. "I didn't hear anything. Did you hear somebody?"

"No. There's a sound outside," Isabel said, closing her eyes so she could hear better. "Shhhh. Listen."

Everybody stopped talking. They could feel a faint vibration below them and to the right, almost like the sound of a large animal groaning.

It was the sound of steel against ice.

ICE

TO THE READER: BEFORE WE CONTINUE WITH THE story, a word or two about icebergs. Now, if you think icebergs are boring, you can skip this part of the book and flip to the end of this chapter, when things get exciting again for the Flashback Four. But you'll be missing out, because icebergs are *very* interesting.

An iceberg isn't just a giant ice cube floating in the ocean. It's not simply water that has frozen. Icebergs are formed as glaciers on the land near the ocean, when snow falls and presses down on top of the layers of snow underneath it. The layers build up over time, sometimes over thousands of years.

Because it's been compacted, the ice in a glacier is harder and much more dense than the ice in your freezer at home. And it's not salty, because it's not made from salt water. When it melts, it becomes clean, fresh water. You could drink it. In fact, it would probably be the purest water you would ever drink.

Very, very slowly, the weight of the glacier causes it to slide toward the edge of the water. Finally, a chunk of it will break off, slip into the ocean, and float away. Each year, forty *thousand* icebergs slide off the coast of Greenland. They get carried by the ocean currents into a part of the north Atlantic known as Iceberg Alley. From there, they float south into warmer water, and they usually melt within a year.

You've probably heard the expression "That's just the tip of the iceberg." What a great expression! It means the problem you see in front of you is only a tiny part of a much larger problem. If you see an iceberg floating in the ocean, you're only seeing the *top* of it. Almost all of it is under the water.

So icebergs can be huge. The largest known iceberg in the Atlantic was the height of a fifty-five-story building. In 1956, there was an iceberg in the Pacific that was larger than Belgium!

Okay, enough with the iceberg trivia. The point is, these things are big, solid, and obviously very dangerous to any ship that's crossing the ocean.

If a shark had attacked the *Titanic*, it wouldn't have made a dent. If Godzilla or King Kong or some horrible movie monster had somehow managed to get loose, swim out into the ocean, and attack the *Titanic*, it wouldn't have been able to do much damage. Just about *anything* could have happened to *Titanic* and the ship would have survived . . . except getting sideswiped for ten seconds by an iceberg.

Let's get back to the Flashback Four, who were locked in a room three levels below deck when the collision took place.

"That's it!" Isabel said, her eyes opened wide. "We hit the iceberg!"

"Are you sure?" asked David, who hadn't heard anything. "How do you know?"

"I can tell," she replied. "I'm sure. Listen."

Ten feet above the ship's keel, the iceberg was still grinding against the hull, popping out the iron rivets and pushing aside the steel plates that made the exterior skin of the *Titanic*. It created a gash three hundred feet long. That's the length of a football field.

Water was pouring in at the rate of a hundred tons per minute. The lowest levels of the *Titanic* were already flooding. The stokers down there who shoveled coal into the boilers were fighting for their lives.

The Flashback Four listened intently, but it was already over. The iceberg had moved on. The damage had been done.

A few seconds later, a gong sounded. This was a warning to the crew that the doors of the watertight compartments had been sealed off. There were sixteen of these on the lower section of *Titanic*. The ship had been designed so that if four of them flooded, *Titanic* would still be able to float for two or three days—enough time for a rescue ship to get there.

Unfortunately, *six* of the watertight compartments had been pierced. That was the tipping point, in more ways than one. *Titanic* was already doomed.

Suddenly, there was absolute quiet. The engines had stopped. Most of the passengers didn't hear or feel the collision with the iceberg, but just about all of them noticed that the constant hum of the engines had stopped. The heartbeat of the *Titanic* was gone. In its place was an eerie silence.

"Okay, now we *really* gotta get out of here!" David said, picking up one of the wooden planks from the bed again. He slammed it against the door with renewed enthusiasm.

"Let us out!" Isabel screamed, pounding on the wall with her fists. "Please! Help! Anybody!"

It was no use. The ship might not have been watertight, but it seemed to be soundproof.

"Nobody's going to rescue us," Luke said. "Our only hope is to break the door down. Come on, maybe if we all hit it at the same time."

The other three each grabbed a wooden plank. Luke and Julia took a position on the right side of the door. David and Isabel moved to the left side of the door so they wouldn't get in one another's way.

"Okay," Luke told the group. "On the count of three, give it all you've got. One . . . two . . . three!"

Bang. Bang. Bang. Bang. Four planks hit the door hard. But it didn't give.

"Again!" Luke hollered. "One . . . two . . . three!"

Bang. Bang. Bang. Bang.

Nothing.

"It's no use," Julia said mournfully. "It's solid."

"One more time!" Luke shouted. "Come on! We can do this! One . . . two . . ."

The door suddenly swung open.

A steward wearing a navy blue White Star Line uniform was standing there. He had a very official-looking cap with a shiny black visor, and a shocked look on his face. Julia, Isabel, Luke, and David were about to swing planks at him.

"What in the blazes are you *doing*?" he asked.

"You saved us!" Isabel said. "Thank you!"

She would have hugged the man, but he now had a very angry look on his face.

"There was a bed in this room," he said, looking around. "I put it here myself. What did you do to it? Did you take it apart?"

"No, it, uh . . . broke," David told him honestly. "When we rammed it into the door."

"You rammed it into the *door*?"

"We were locked in," Julia explained. "We were trying to get out."

"That bed was the property of the White Star Line!" the steward shouted. "You can't go around destroying private property! It's against the law."

"Mr. Astor told us this is international waters," said David. "So we can do anything we want."

"You don't understand," Isabel tried to explain to the steward. "You see—"

"I'm going to report this to my superior," he said. "The four of you will be arrested as soon as we get to New York."

He tried to close the door to lock them in again,

but Luke—thinking quickly—jammed his foot in the doorway to prevent the door from closing. He wasn't about to get stuck in that room again.

"I've got news for you, pal," Luke told the steward through the crack in the doorway. "This ship will never make it to New York. We just hit an iceberg. Soon, *all* of this will be at the bottom of the ocean. Including your bed."

"Don't be ridiculous," the steward replied. "We're making excellent time. We're scheduled to arrive in New York the day after tomorrow."

"Look, we don't have time to argue," David said, pushing the door open all the way. "Let's go!"

They shoved the steward out of the way, and the Flashback Four dashed through the open doorway.

"I'm reporting you kids!" the steward shouted as they ran down the hallway.

"You do that!" Luke hollered.

IT'S HAPPENING

"SO LONG, SUCKER!" DAVID YELLED, CACKLING AS the Flashback Four ran down the hallway.

There was really no cause for celebration. It was past midnight now. In about two hours, the mighty *Titanic* would break into two enormous pieces and sink beneath the ocean, eventually coming to rest two miles below on the floor of the Atlantic. Fifteen hundred people were going to lose their lives. But David couldn't resist having a little fun, after being cooped up in that dismal room for so long.

By this time, the captain of the *Titanic*—Edward John Smith—had been awakened by the crew and told the ship had struck an iceberg. He didn't know the extent of the damage yet, but he knew it was serious, and he didn't waste a minute. Smith issued an order to call for help over the wireless radio, a new technology in 1912. Then he quickly put on his full captain's uniform—brass buttons, gold lace stripes, black tie— and rushed to the bridge.

Smith, who was sixty-two years old, with white hair and a neatly trimmed beard, was a dashing figure. He had been a British Naval Reserve captain for twenty-five years. He was planning to retire after the *Titanic*'s maiden voyage. So much for that idea.

Luke, Julia, Isabel, and David ran down the hallway and climbed the first flight of stairs they saw, turning around to make sure the steward wasn't chasing them. David's watch was broken, of course, and all four of them had lost track of the time while they were locked up.

"I thought you said I wouldn't have to run!" Isabel shouted as she struggled to make her way up the steps in her long dress.

"Hurry! We've got to get up on deck!" Luke shouted back.

"I hope we can still make it to the meeting spot in time," Julia said.

"Is the camera ready?" David asked Luke. "Are you ready to take the shot?"

"I'm ready!" Luke called back, out of breath now.

As they passed one of the starboard decks on the stairs, they stopped for a moment. There were big chunks of ice scattered across the floor. Obviously, they had been chipped off the iceberg as it went by. A group of young boys were kicking them around like they were soccer balls. A couple of teenagers were making snowballs out of the ice chunks and throwing them at each other.

"Shut the dampers!" one of the crew members hollered through a megaphone. "Draw the fires!"

When the Flashback Four finally got up to the main

deck, members of the crew were removing the canvas covers from the lifeboats. They worked quickly but quietly, as if they didn't want the passengers to know what they were doing.

"What's going on?" an elderly gentleman wearing a bowler hat asked one of the crew members.

"This is just a precaution, sir," he was told. "Nothing to concern yourself about."

Isabel desperately wanted to tell the man, "Don't believe him! The ship is going to sink! Make sure you get into a lifeboat! Save yourself!"

But she didn't. The last time they tried telling the truth about what was going to happen, they were locked up and left to die.

There were more people up on deck now than earlier. Word of the collision had passed around the ship like a game of telephone. Everybody knew that something had happened involving an iceberg, but nobody knew exactly what. Smiling gawkers poured out of the stairways and elevators to see what all the fuss was about. Some of them were carrying binoculars. It was like they were going on a whale-watching expedition.

"Ooh, I've never seen an iceberg before!" an old lady told her friend excitedly.

"Neither have I."

And they never *would* see one. The iceberg that had sideswiped the *Titanic* was already half a mile behind the ship. It was huge, but it was too dark to see it on a moonless night—which is one reason why *Titanic* had collided with it in the first place. If the moon had been full, the lookouts would have seen the iceberg from much farther away, and maybe the ship could have been steered around it.

To the Flashback Four, the amazing thing was that everything on deck seemed so . . . normal. People weren't running around hysterically or tearfully hugging their children one last time. They had no idea that the ship was going to sink. Everybody was just laughing, drinking, and chatting as they strolled the deck or looked out over the rail trying to catch a glimpse of the iceberg.

"I feel like we should *do* something," Isabel told the others, "or tell somebody."

"What's the point?" David asked. "There's nothing we can do now. It's too late to prevent the ship from hitting the iceberg. The damage is done."

"And if we start telling them what's going to happen next," Luke added, "they might lock us up for good this time."

"Then we need to take the photo," Julia suggested. "At least Miss Z can't accuse us of coming home without getting the shot."

"Take a photo of *what*?" David asked. "The ship isn't even tilted in the water yet. Miss Z specifically told us to take a picture of the *Titanic* as it's sinking."

"It *is* sinking!" Julia replied. "But none of these people know it yet."

"What if it sinks really *suddenly*?" Isabel asked. "It could go under at any moment. Then we're dead unless we're at the meeting spot. We don't even have life preservers. I'm going to text Miss Z."

She pulled out the TTT and typed this simple message . . .

HIT BERG

A minute or so later, this response came back . . .

PERFECT

Isabel texted back . . .

EVERYTHING LOOKS NORMAL. SHIP DOES NOT LOOK LIKE IT'S SINKING.

Miss Z replied . . .

IT WILL. IT WILL TAKE A WHILE FOR THE HULL TO FILL WITH WATER. WHAT TIME IS IT THERE?

A man was walking by briskly with a little dog on a leash. Isabel ran over to him.

"Excuse me," she said. "Can you please tell me the hour?"

"Certainly," the man replied, taking out his pocket watch. "It's fifteen minutes past midnight."

Isabel texted, IT'S 12:15.

Miss Z replied, RELAX. U HAVE PLENTY OF TIME. SHIP GOES UNDER AT 2:20.

Less than two hours. Not a lot of time, really. A great blast of steam blew out one of *Titanic*'s enormous funnels. Water had swamped one of the ship's boilers.

"Relax, she says," muttered Isabel. "How can I relax when I know what's going to happen?"

"It's all good," David said. "There's nothing we can do but wait. Then we'll take the picture and get out of here."

Water poured in through the lower part of the *Titanic*, of course, below the water line. So it was the lowest levels of the ship that were flooding first. Coincidentally, that's where the poorest passengers and crew members were.

Laborers—the stokers and greasers who worked in the engine room—would be the first to die. They had no escape route.

Above them was the part of the ship that was called "steerage." It was filled with hundreds of immigrants who had left England, Ireland, and other countries to find new hope for a better life in America. Many of them saved money all their lives to afford the thirty-five-dollar ticket to cross the ocean. Some of them saw a toilet for the first time on the *Titanic*.

The steerage class was pretty much treated like cattle. Iron gates prevented those people from mixing with the first-class passengers. The gates also prevented them from escaping the water, which had already covered the floor of their deck and was rising fast. People in steerage were starting to panic.

But up on the top deck, where the wealthy had paid $430 for their tickets, it was like any other night on a cruise ship. People were just milling around, chatting and laughing as if nothing unusual was happening.

The Flashback Four were tired, and it was late. With nothing to do but wait for the inevitable, they wandered into the first-class dining lounge, which extended across the full width of the ship, to get out of the cold and sit down for a while.

The lounge was opulent, with deep pile carpets and white tablecloths. The room was decorated with crystal chandeliers, silk upholstered chairs, elegant curtains, walnut wood paneling, and potted palm trees. And lots of rich people.

"I feel like I should be wearing a tuxedo or something," Luke said, pulling his RMS *Titanic* bathrobe around him.

"You look fine," Julia told him. "Rich people are *allowed* to walk around in public wearing bathrobes. That just makes them a little eccentric. When poor people walk around in bathrobes, that means they're crazy."

The lounge was connected to Café Parisien, one of the five restaurants on board. Luke picked up a menu that had been left on the table. Oysters . . . saute of chicken Lyonnaise . . . roast squab . . . pâté de foie gras. He had never even *heard* of most of the foods before.

"People actually *eat* this stuff?" he asked.

"I'm getting hungry," Julia said. "We should have brought protein bars or something with us."

"I'd eat *anything* at this point," David said.

There was a four-piece band in a corner of the lounge. They picked up their instruments and began playing a popular song of the era, "Shine On, Harvest Moon." Moments later a waiter came over, carrying a little note pad and pencil in his hands.

"May I help you?" he asked in a British accent.

The kids glanced at each other. None of them had any money.

"Uh, no thanks," Isabel told the waiter. "Would it be okay if we just hung out here for a while?"

"Feel free to dangle from the ceiling if you'd like," the waiter replied, just a little snootily. Then he walked away.

A well-dressed young couple came in and sat down at the table to the right. The woman took out a cigarette and her husband reached over to light it for her, just like in the old movies. The Flashback Four watched with curiosity and some amount of disgust. None of them had ever seen anyone smoke indoors before. Isabel coughed.

"Isn't this exciting, darling?" the woman said, blowing a smoke ring.

"What is?" her husband asked. He was distracted, snapping his fingers in an effort to get the attention of the waiter.

"The iceberg, silly!" she replied. "We apparently bumped against it. Our honeymoon has been such a dead bore. But now I'll have a story to tell the girls when we get to New York."

"That's for sure," Isabel whispered, coughing again from the smoke.

The rest of the Flashback Four kept their mouths shut, flashing nervous looks back and forth. Finally, the waiter came over to the couple's table.

"My good man," the husband said, "bring us a bottle of your finest wine, will you? And fetch me a piece of ice from that iceberg we bumped. We can put it in our drinks."

"Very good, sir," the waiter said before leaving.

"What a marvelous idea, darling!" said the woman. "We'll toast the iceberg."

The Flashback Four rolled their eyes and tried not to laugh.

"These people are oblivious," whispered Isabel.

"What does *that* mean?" Luke asked.

"It means they have no idea what's about to hit them."

The band finished playing the song and immediately launched into a jaunty version of "Alexander's Ragtime Band." When the waiter arrived with a bottle of wine and glasses full of ice, the young couple took them outside so they could propose a toast to the iceberg out on the deck.

Their table stayed vacant for a few minutes, until

another couple approached. The Flashback Four had to look at the man for a few seconds until one by one they realized he had a familiar face.

It was John Jacob Astor IV.

"Run!" David said, getting up from his seat to bolt out of there.

Astor held up his hand. He had a smile on his face.

"Please," he said, "sit down. Relax. I mean you no harm. In fact, I admire the resourcefulness you displayed to get out of that, shall I say, *predicament* you were in. We need more young people like that. I should hire you to work for my company. I don't believe I caught your names when we first met."

"Isabel."

"Julia."

"Luke."

"David."

Each one shook the famous man's hand.

This time Astor was not with his entourage or bodyguards. He was with his wife. She was only nineteen years old, and noticeably pregnant. They were coming home after their honeymoon in Europe and Egypt.

"And this lovely lady is my bride, Madeleine," Astor said.

"Charmed, I'm sure," she said, looking totally bored.

The waiter rushed over, bowing to Astor as if he was the king of England. Astor told him they were not hungry and just wanted to sit for a while. Then he leaned over to the Flashback Four.

"Tell me," he whispered, "how did you know? About the iceberg, I mean."

"Do you want to know the truth?" David asked.

"The whole truth and nothing but the truth," Astor replied, raising his right hand.

"Okay," David said. "Here's what happened . . ."

He proceeded to tell Astor and his wife the story of how Miss Z created the Board to send people through time, and how they had been recruited to be the Flashback Four. Madeleine was disinterested, but Astor hung on every word, especially when Luke got to the part about the *Titanic* sinking.

"Fascinating!" he said when David had finished. "Mind you, I don't believe a word of it. But you tell a marvelous tale! This ship is unsinkable, young man. Everyone knows that."

"Wanna bet?" David asked.

"I'd wager two thousand dollars that your story is

fabricated," Astor replied. "But I doubt you have the funds to make a bet."

"Well, you're right about that," David admitted.

"Please don't tell that tale to the other passengers," Astor whispered. "You don't want to set off a panic."

He turned away from the Flashback Four to whisper a few sweet nothings in the ear of his young bride. But curiosity must have gotten the better of him, because a minute later he turned back.

"Tell me something," he said to David. "You claim you can predict what's going to happen before it happens. So if you know so much, can you tell me who's going to win the World Series this year?"

"Uhh . . ."

David looked at him blankly. So did the girls. David tried to come up with reasons why he didn't know the winner of the 1912 World Series. That was more than a hundred years ago, in his world. How could he possibly be expected to know?

"If you *truly* come from the future," said Astor, "you should know who won the World Series, am I right?"

"I'm not really a baseball fan," said Julia.

"Can we go now, sweetie?" Astor's wife asked impatiently. "I'm cold."

Suddenly Luke stood up triumphantly. "The Red Sox won it!" he said, holding up his hand to get a high five from David.

Luke was right. Every serious Red Sox fan knows that Boston was a baseball powerhouse during this era, winning the World Series in 1912, 1915, 1916, and 1918. After that came the *long* dry spell when they didn't win a championship again until 2004.

"The Sox are gonna beat the Giants four games to three," Luke told Astor. "Smoky Joe Wood's gonna win two games. And that last game at Fenway Park is gonna go into extra innings."

"You don't say?" Astor said, impressed. "You seem pretty sure of yourself."

"Oh, you can bet on it, Mr. Astor," Luke told him. "Take it to the bank. Go make yourself another fortune."

"I just might do that," Astor whispered. Then he pulled out his wallet, peeled off a bill and pressed it into Luke's hand. "For now, we must take our leave."

"It was nice meeting you," Isabel said as Astor and his wife got up.

"Charmed, I'm sure," said Mrs. Astor.

As soon as they were gone, David, Julia, and Isabel were all over Luke.

"Why'd you tell him all that stuff about the World

Series, dude?" David said.

"Now he's gonna bet on the Red Sox to win," Isabel said. "He's gonna make millions!"

"We're not supposed to change history, remember?" added Julia.

"I'm not changing history," Luke explained. "He's not going to be betting on anybody. In a couple of hours, he's going to be dead. Remember?"

"Oh yeah."

Luke opened up the bill that Astor had slipped into his hand. It was a hundred dollars.

"Whoa!" Isabel exclaimed. "A hundred bucks?"

"Are you kidding me?" said David.

"He gave you a C-note?" asked Julia. "What are you going to do with it?"

Luke thought about it for a moment. Then he stood up.

"Waiter!" Luke called, snapping his fingers.

The waiter came over. He still had that snooty look on his face.

"I thought you just wanted to . . . hang around," he said.

"We changed our minds," Luke told him, waving the bill in the air. "What can we order for a hundred dollars?"

The waiter examined the bill, as if he didn't think it could possibly be real.

"For a hundred dollars," he finally said, "you can order everything on the menu."

"Then that's what we'll have," Luke said. "Bring us everything on the menu, my good man! And make it snappy. My friends are very hungry."

"Very good, sir," the waiter said, bowing deeply.

It wasn't long before he and a few other waiters were back, carrying big platters full of food. The Flashback Four feasted on lobster thermidor, quail's eggs in aspic with caviar, poached salmon with dilled mousseline sauce, and other fancy fare that rich people enjoyed. They ate with silver-plated cutlery and drank from cut crystal glassware.

The best part was that there was still enough money left over to get dessert, so the kids ordered raspberry white chocolate mousse, flambéd vanilla-poached pears with apricot sauce, Sicilian ricotta cheescake, and just to be on the safe side, various puddings and French ice cream.

"This is *amazing*," Julia said, stuffing her face.

"I could get used to this," added Isabel.

For a brief moment, they were able to forget they were on a ship that would very shortly be at the bottom of the Atlantic Ocean. When the meal was over, David could barely move back from the table.

"This is the best meal I've ever had in my life," he said. "I think I'm gonna throw up."

The sumptuous feast ended when a steward burst into the lounge with a megaphone.

"All passengers on deck, with life belts on," he announced. "Repeat. All passengers on deck *immediately* with life belts on."

The passengers in the lounge were not happy that their meals had been interrupted.

"What's going on?" a white-haired man asked.

"It's just an exercise, sir," the steward told him. "Nothing to be alarmed about."

"An exercise at *this* hour?" somebody else grumbled. "That's preposterous!"

"It's outrageous!" a matronly lady said. "I'm going to write a strongly worded letter of complaint to the White Star Line. They can't treat us like this."

"I paid good money for this trip!" somebody else said as they stormed out of the lounge.

"It's happening," Isabel whispered to the others as they got up from their seats. "We'd better get out of here."

While the stewards were reassuring passengers

that everything was fine, telegraphers in the radio room were furiously tapping out this message . . .

. . . − − − . . .

. . . − − − . . .

Three dots represents the letter *S*. Three dashes represents the letter *O*. SOS. Save Our Ship. Or sometimes, Save Our Souls.

By this time, Captain Smith had assessed the damage. He knew the *Titanic* was going down, and he knew it wouldn't be long. He gave the order to signal other ships in the area to come quickly. But he didn't want the passengers to panic.

The Flashback Four left the lounge and went out on the deck. There was a flurry of activity out there now. People were milling around, some of them wearing pajamas and many of them wearing life jackets. Just about all of them looked sleepy and confused.

"Nothing to be alarmed about," a member of the crew announced. "We're just taking a few safety precautions."

"You woke us from a good night's sleep for *this*?" complained a woman holding her crying baby.

Just then, another cloud of steam blasted out of

the ship's funnels. One of the boilers down below had flooded with ice-cold salt water.

Suddenly, a small rocket shot high in the air and exploded with a bang and a burst of bright blue light. Everyone stopped what they were doing to stare up at the sky. Even the babies stopped crying to get a look.

But this wasn't the start of a fireworks show for the amusement of the children on board. It was a distress rocket, fired in the hope that somebody, *anybody*, on another ship would see it and come to the rescue.

There was no hiding the truth now. *Titanic* was sinking, and everybody on board knew it.

"Get on your life vests!" shouted a steward urgently. "There's trouble ahead!"

ALL HANDS ON DECK

IT WAS APRIL 15 NOW, AND ALMOST ONE O'CLOCK in the morning.

For the first time, passengers on board the *Titanic* could tell the ship was tilted. They could feel something was crooked as they walked along the deck. They could see it, too. The bow was dipping forward and to the right ever so slightly as seawater filled the lower levels and kept rushing in. It was like when you pour water into an ice cube tray and watch it spill over into the other little squares as it tilts.

A whistle above blew. People were streaming up on the deck by the hundreds now. Some of them were dressed in their evening gowns and fancy finery. Others had on bathrobes or were wrapped in blankets.

Some wore boots, and others went barefoot. Nobody had time to get properly dressed. Some carried little dogs or half-asleep children in their arms.

But all the passengers had one thing in common as they stepped out on the deck—a look of confusion in their eyes. Those who had slept through the initial collision had no idea why the stewards had rushed from cabin to cabin, banging on doors and yelling for everyone to come up on deck right away.

Gradually, the realization was setting in that something was terribly wrong. But there wasn't a full-scale panic. Not yet. It was just too hard for people to comprehend that the "unsinkable" *Titanic* was actually sinking.

The musicians had been quietly instructed to leave the first-class lounge and go out on deck to play happy music and keep the passengers calm. They set up their instruments and began playing "Oh, You Beautiful Doll."

"Everyone up on deck with life belts on!" the stewards hollered through cupped hands. "Hurry! Hurry!"

"Why do we need to wear life belts?" a grandfatherly-looking gentleman complained. "I thought they said this ship was unsinkable."

"Are we sinking?" asked a frightened lady.

"Of course not, ma'am," a steward assured her. "Everything will be fine."

"You disturbed my sleep for *this*?" another man complained. "I have a mind to report you, young man."

The Flashback Four elbowed their way through the crowd on the deck, trying to move toward the front of the ship.

"This is it," David whispered to the others. "This is when it all goes down."

"In more ways than one," Luke whispered back. "Let's get to the meeting spot, take the picture, and blow out of here. Isabel, maybe you should tell Miss Z what's happening so she'll be ready to get us."

They moved off to the side for a moment, where passengers were already being escorted into lifeboats, which were lined up along the rail. For a second, the thought crossed Isabel's mind that maybe they should get *into* a lifeboat. If anything went wrong with Miss Z and the Board, at least they would survive.

On the other hand, if they got into a lifeboat now, they could forget about ever going back home to Boston. They would have to live the rest of their lives in the wrong century.

STARTING TO FILL LIFEBOATS, Isabel texted.

While she waited for a response from Miss Z, the

Flashback Four watched the crew members struggle to maneuver the lifeboat in front of them, which was hanging from thick ropes over the deck. The boat was surprisingly large, about thirty feet long. The White Star Line emblem was on the side.

There were sixteen lifeboats, eight lined up on each side of *Titanic*, plus four "collapsible" lifeboats that had canvas sides. Each boat could hold sixty-five people.

The ship's designer had recommended that *Titanic* carry forty-eight lifeboats, which would have held more than three thousand people. That would have been plenty to save all the passengers and crew.

I don't need to do the math for you. Twenty lifeboats was not *nearly* enough. Most of the people on board would not make it, including fifty-two children.

Why didn't *Titanic* carry enough lifeboats? Because somebody—and nobody knows who—decided that forty-eight lifeboats would make the deck of the ship look too crowded. The first-class passengers would not be able to promenade down the deck so easily in their fancy clothes. That would go down in history as one of the dumbest mistakes ever.

Finally, Miss Z sent a text back . . .

WHATEVER YOU DO, DON'T GET ON A LIFEBOAT.

"If we get on a boat, she won't be able to bring us back," Isabel reminded the others.

A few people had lined up in front of the nearest boat with their life jackets on. There was no mad dash, no panic. It almost looked like they were lining up to take a leisurely boat ride.

"Women and children first," shouted one of the crew members. "Ladies, you may board at this time. Watch your step."

This was the age of chivalry, when men opened doors for women and placed jackets over puddles so "the fairer sex" would not have to get their dainty feet wet. As a result, most of the women on the *Titanic* would survive. Only one out of every five male passengers would be alive the next day.

"We'll see you later," a few husbands said as their wives stepped into the lifeboat and kissed them good-bye. But they never would.

"Plenty of room," hollered the steward who was helping to load the boat. "Who's next?"

Some people were standing around watching, but only a few of them stepped forward. The lifeboat was only about half full.

"Hey, you kids," the steward shouted at the Flash-back Four. "There's still room for you in this boat.

Right up front. Hop in. Quickly."

"No, thank you," Julia told him. "We have other plans."

"Suit yourself," he replied, escorting a few more ladies on board. He tossed a sack of biscuits and emergency supplies into the boat, and then shouted, "Okay, boys, let this one go!"

For reasons that were never quite explained, many of the lifeboats on the *Titanic* were launched with less than the maximum capacity of sixty-five passengers. The crew members were in a hurry to get the boats into the water before the ship sank, of course, but there was really no excuse for releasing lifeboats that were just half full. One boat only had *twelve* people in it. Hundreds more lives could have been saved if all the lifeboats had been filled to capacity. It was one of those many mysteries of the *Titanic*.

Hanging from a rope at each end, the boat was lowered in a jerky fashion, first one side and then the other. Each time a part of the boat jerked down, the women and children in it would scream. It looked like the whole thing might flip over and throw them all into the water.

"Okay, cut the rope!" a crew member shouted once the boat was low enough. Somebody produced a knife, and after a bit of sawing, the boat splashed into the water below.

The Flashback Four were not the only ones who turned down the chance to get in a lifeboat. As they made their way up the deck past the next boat, many of the women and children standing there were refusing to climb into it.

"I'll stay where I am, thank you very much," said a well-dressed lady. "I feel a lot safer right here than I would be on that little wooden dinghy."

Another woman was about to step into the lifeboat when she suddenly changed her mind. "I'm afraid of boats!" she screamed, crying and struggling to climb back on the ship.

"Madam, what do you think *Titanic* is?" asked the steward who was trying to assist her.

The crew was faced with a very difficult job. They were trying to keep everyone calm, but at the same time get everyone off the doomed ship as quickly as possible. And of course, they had their own lives to worry about too.

"Where is my husband?" begged a crying woman in the lifeboat as she grabbed the sleeve of a steward. "Will there be another boat for the men?"

"Don't worry, ma'am, everything will be fine," he

assured her. "We're using the wireless to contact other ships in the vicinity right now. One will be along very soon to pick up your husband. And *Titanic* can float for several days, even if she is badly damaged."

It was a lie, of course. The truth was that *Titanic* would be completely underwater in less than an hour. The nearest ship—the *Californian*—was two hours away, and it wasn't responding to the distress signals anyway. The nearest ship that *did* reply to the signal— the *Carpathia*—was fifty-eight miles away. That may seem quite close, but the *Carpathia* had a maximum speed of just seventeen miles an hour. It would take more than three hours to get there.

As the *Titanic* tilted forward inch by inch, the musicians continued playing popular tunes of the day . . .

"Glow little glow worm,
glow and glimmer
Swim through the sea of night,
little swimmer . . ."

Only one more lifeboat stood between the Flashback Four and their meeting spot at the bow of the ship. A steward was trying to convince an older woman with an enormous hat to get into the boat, but she was resisting.

"Leave me be, young man!" she yelled at him, pulling her arm away. "I will *not* be separated from my husband."

Her husband stood at the rail helplessly, shaking his head from side to side. His name was Isidor Straus, and while you probably don't know that name, he was quite well-known in his day. Straus was the co-owner of Macy's, the famous department store in New York. His wife, Ida, pushed the steward away and climbed back on deck.

"As we have lived," she said, "so will we die— together."

The Flashback Four watched Mr. and Mrs. Straus, fascinated.

"That's the most romantic thing I ever saw," Julia said, wiping away a tear.

The steward didn't give up easily. He knew who the Strauses were, and wanted very much to save their lives.

"I'll make room for you too, Mr. Straus," he said. "One seat for each of you. You can be together."

"I will *not* go before the other men," Mr. Straus replied gallantly, and then he turned on his heel and walked away with his wife, arm in arm.

The couple would perish together.

At that moment another couple hurried over to the lifeboat. It was John Jacob Astor and his young wife, Madeleine. This time they had their little dog with them, an Airedale terrier named Kitty. The steward helped Mrs. Astor onto the boat, but put his hand up to prevent Mr. Astor from taking the seat next to her.

"My wife is in a delicate condition," Astor explained to the steward. "Perhaps I should be with her."

"I'm sorry, sir," said the steward, who obviously

didn't recognize one of the richest men in the world. "No men *or dogs* are allowed in these boats until the women and children are loaded on first."

Astor flashed a look of anger for a moment, and then resignation.

"Don't worry about me, dear," he called to his wife. "I will get a seat in another boat. I will meet you when we get to New York."

Before leaving, Astor pulled off his fur-lined gloves and tossed them, underhand, to his wife.

"These will keep you warm, dear," he said.

"Good-bye, sweetheart," she replied.

They would never see each other again.

As he was walking away with tears in his eyes, John Jacob Astor spotted the Flashback Four off to the side and went right over to them.

"Tell me again how you knew," he asked the group. "How did you know the ship was going to strike an iceberg? How did you know it would sink?"

"We told you," Luke replied. "We came here from the future with a smartboard that can send people through time."

"I didn't believe you," Astor said. "Now I do."

Mr. Astor was about to walk away, but then he stopped and turned around one more time.

"So the Boston Red Sox really *are* going to win the World Series, aren't they?" he asked.

Luke nodded his head.

"Tell me something," Astor said. "Is this my last night on earth?"

Luke didn't know what to say. He looked at David, Julia, and Isabel for advice, but they just shrugged. How do you tell a man he's going to die in an hour? Luke didn't want to answer, so he just kept his eyes on the floor.

"Mr. Astor, we wanted to thank you for the money you gave us," Julia said, changing the subject. "We had quite a feast, thanks to you."

"It was nothing," Astor said with a sigh. Then he took his wallet from his pocket, pulled out a wad of bills, and handed them to Julia. "Here. I guess you won this fair and square. I won't be needing it anymore."

Then he turned around and walked away slowly.

Julia almost fainted as she counted the money. Twenty bills, each one of them a hundred.

"It's two *thousand* dollars!" she said. "Do you have any idea what two thousand dollars could buy in 1912?"

"It's not going to buy *anything* if we don't get out of here," Luke said.

"What time is it?" Isabel asked, fully aware that

none of them had a working watch. And with the ship about to sink, it didn't seem appropriate to stop somebody and ask the time of day.

"Come *on*," David urged. "It doesn't matter what time it is. We gotta get to the meeting spot."

Julia stashed the bills in her pocket. In Isabel's pocket, the TTT buzzed. There was a message from Miss Z . . .

HOW DOES IT LOOK? ARE YOU READY TO TAKE THE PICTURE?

Luke took out the camera and looked around. The deck was definitely tilted. People were hustling around in the background. It wouldn't be a great picture of the ship actually sinking, but it would have to do. If they waited until the last minute to snap a picture, it might be too late.

"Tell her I'm about to shoot it," Luke told Isabel as he got down on one knee to improve the angle and steady himself.

This was the whole reason they had accepted the mission—to take a photo of the *Titanic* as it was sinking. It would be the *only* photo of its kind in the world. Luke had to get it right.

But as he was about to push the shutter, two stewards grabbed David and Julia by their arms.

"You kids!" one of them yelled. "What are you

standing around here for? You should be in the boats!"

"Where are your life jackets?" shouted the other one. "Every cabin has life jackets. Where are yours?"

There was no time to fool around. David punched one of the stewards with his free hand and Julia kneed the other one in the groin. Isabel started kicking and Luke got up to help his friends.

"Leave us *alone*!" Julia screamed, poking one of the stewards in the eye. "We're *not* getting into a lifeboat, so buzz off!"

The "fight" didn't last long. If people don't want to be saved, you can't force them.

"Have it your way!" one of the stewards shouted. "You can die here if you want to!"

The Flashback Four ran away, rushing toward the meeting spot at front of the ship. Time was running short now. The water was starting to lap across parts of the deck, so it was getting wet and slippery. And the water was *cold*, below freezing. Patches of ice were forming here and there.

"Don't stop and talk to *anybody*," Luke said as they ran. "We're running out of time!"

As they neared the front of the ship, it became obvious that choosing the bow as their meeting spot had been a mistake. The front of the ship filled with water first, so it was tilting *down*. It would have been smarter to pick a meeting spot at the *back* of the ship, which was tilting up.

"Whose bright idea was *this*?" asked David after he almost slipped on some ice. "The meeting spot might be underwater at this point!"

"I don't know," replied Julia, who knew very well that meeting at the bow had been her idea.

"Miss Z should have known," Isabel said as she struggled to catch up to the others. "She should have told us. It's her fault."

"It doesn't *matter* whose fault it is," Luke said. "Let's go!"

Finally, after traveling the entire length of the huge ship, the Flashback Four reached the bow—the meeting spot. It was still above water, but just barely.

"That's it!" Isabel shouted, pointing at the railing she remembered from the movie. "That's the spot where Jack said he was king of the world!"

"We're going to be saved!" Julia shouted gleefully.

Unfortunately, there was an obstacle in front of the meeting spot. It was a guy, a big guy with big muscles. He wasn't wearing a White Star Line uniform. He looked like a bouncer. His arms were folded in front of his chest, and he didn't look very happy.

"Run along, you kids," he said with a gruff Irish accent. "This part of the ship is off limits to passengers. There are lifeboats at the port side. If you hurry, you can still get into one of them."

"Oh man," David mumbled wearily to Luke, "are we going to have to fight *this* guy now?"

"It's two against one," Luke whispered back. "He's big, but we can take him. You go for his legs and I'll take care of the rest."

But before they could start the big fight, Julia stepped forward. She did a curtsy in front of the big man, a smile on her face.

"My name is Julia Brennan," she said. "What is your name, sir?"

"Thomas Maloney," he grunted.

"Mr. Maloney, my friends and I just want to snap a photo. You know, so we'll have a little souvenir of our trip on the *Titanic*."

"This is no time to be taking pictures," Mr. Maloney told her. "It's very dangerous here. You could get washed overboard."

"We know. We're being very careful," Julia replied politely as she reached into her pocket. "Tell me something, Mr. Maloney. If I gave you this, would you let us take a picture?"

She peeled off ten bills and handed them to Mr. Maloney. He looked at them, counted them, then looked up at Julia with astonishment.

"You're gonna give me a thousand bucks to let you take a *picture*?" Maloney asked. The angry look had left his face and suddenly he was all smiles.

"Yes," Julia told him, "if you'll pose for it."

"Go right ahead," he replied. "Take all the pictures you want."

"Great," Julia said. "Okay Luke, you take the picture. Isabel, maybe you should tell Miss Z it's time to pick us up."

While Luke set up the shot with Mr. Maloney, Isabel discreetly pulled out the TTT. She texted, WE R READY TO BE PICKED UP.

Luke got down on one knee and instructed Mr. Maloney to stand in front of the railing. It would be the perfect shot. Water was already creeping up on deck and the bottom of the rail was submerged.

"Smile!" Luke instructed.

Mr. Maloney smiled.

At that moment, the front of the ship abruptly lurched down a foot or so, sending everyone sprawling. Water splashed across the bow. Mr. Maloney grabbed on to the railing to avoid falling overboard.

So did David. Luke bobbled the camera, nearly drop-ping it in the water.

As Isabel fell down, the TTT slipped out of her hand and slid forward across the slippery bow. She desperately reached out to retrieve it, but the TTT fell into the ocean.

KING OF THE WORLD

DID U SHOOT THE PHOTO? MISS Z TEXTED, USING THE COM-puter on her desk.

It was not yet 2:05, the time she had agreed to pick up the Flashback Four. She wanted to make sure they got the picture before she brought them back home.

Miss Z waited a few seconds for a response. When it didn't come, she texted again.

REPEAT. DID U GET THE SHOT?

No response.

Miss Z called over her assistant, Mrs. Vader, for help as she fiddled with the computer. Up until this moment, Isabel had been very prompt in replying to every text. Maybe something was wrong with the TTT, Miss Z thought.

ARE U THERE? she texted.

Nothing.

"Kids!" said Mrs. Vader. "If they don't want to communicate, they just don't. My son does the same thing. It's their way of having some control over authority figures."

"Something might be wrong out there," said Miss Z, in perhaps the understatement of the year. She had no idea that the TTT, which she had spent a billion dollars developing, was at that moment sinking down to the bottom of the Atlantic Ocean.

WFRE ARE U? she texted so quickly that she misspelled words. ANSER PLEEASE.

"I know it's early, but maybe you should think about bringing them back *now*," Mrs. Vader suggested. "Just to be on the safe side."

"I was thinking the same thing."

Miss Z fired up the Board and quickly tapped out a series of commands on her computer. After a few seconds, the Board buzzed and lit up in a flash of bright blue. The blue screen split into five bands of color, and then they merged together to form a single band of bright white light. There was something beautiful about it.

"Let's hope this works," Miss Z said, as the room

was filled with an intense humming sound. "I wasn't planning to bring them back until five minutes after two. But I'm worried about them. Those kids are my responsibility."

Mrs. Vader crossed her fingers. After a few more seconds, the screen began to flicker. An image began to appear.

"It's working!" shouted Mrs. Vader.

The image on the screen flickered faster and faster, and then there was a bright white flash. When it went out, there was one lone figure standing in front of the Board.

Thomas Maloney.

The big man landed on his feet and shook his head, as if he had just woken up from an intense dream.

Mrs. Vader screamed.

"Who are *you*?" shouted Miss Z.

"My name is Thomas Maloney," he replied as he looked around the room. "I might ask the same question of you, ma'am. And where am I? What am I doing here?"

"Mr. Maloney, were you on the *Titanic* just a minute ago?" asked Miss Z.

"I sure was," he replied. "And she was sinkin' fast."

"Well, we just saved your life," Miss Z told him.

"You're probably the luckiest man in the world."

"I don't feel lucky. Where am I?"

"You are in Boston, Massachusetts, Mr. Maloney," said Mrs. Vader.

"That's most amusing, ma'am," he said, chuckling.

"We're dead serious," said Miss Z. "This is the twenty-first century."

"Twenty-*first*? That's impossible," Maloney said. "This is 1912. Everybody knows that. You must be mixed up in the head, lady. What is *that* thing?"

"It's called a computer," explained Miss Z. "It's interfaced with the smartboard behind you. That's what I used to bring you here."

"Interfaced?" Maloney said. "I never seen one of them contraptions before."

"Who cares about that?" shouted Mrs. Vader. "What about the *kids*?"

"Mr. Maloney, when you were on the *Titanic*, did you happen to see four children, about twelve years old?" asked Miss Z. "Two boys, two girls? One of the boys is African American?"

"African American? What's that mean?" Maloney replied. "But yeah, I was talkin' with four kids just before this happened."

"Where were they?" asked Mrs. Vader.

"They were standin' right in front of me a minute ago," he said, "at the very front of the ship. They were takin' my picture. They even gave me a thousand bucks to do it. And the next thing I knew . . . I was here. I guess they must still be there."

Mr. Maloney pulled the bills out of his pocket and showed them to Miss Z.

"This is bad," Miss Z said, furiously typing on her keyboard. "This is *very* bad."

On the *Titanic*, the Flashback Four were in full-scale panic mode.

"No!" Isabel shrieked, reaching into the water in a desperate attempt to grab the TTT.

It was no use. The TTT was gone. There would be no way for them to communicate with Miss Z anymore.

Furthermore, Mr. Maloney was gone. One moment he had been in front of them posing for a picture, and the next moment he had disappeared. He didn't fall overboard. He just vanished. The Flashback Four were in shock.

"Did you see *that*?" asked David, rubbing his eyes.

"He's gone!" shouted Julia. "Where did he go?"

"Miss Z must have zapped *him* back instead of us," Luke guessed.

"What are we supposed to do *now*?" asked Isabel, her eyes filling with tears. "We can't talk with her. It's all my fault. Now we're stuck here. We gave up our spots on a lifeboat. We don't even have life jackets. I *knew* we shouldn't have come here. Now we're going to *die* here!"

Isabel collapsed into full-blown, shoulder-heaving, blubbering sobs. Julia put an arm around her to comfort her, but soon she was crying too. David was doing his best to fight back tears.

By all rights, this is where the story of the Flashback Four should come to an end. But you've probably noticed there are a few more chapters left in this book.

CHAPTER 12

EVERY MAN FOR HIMSELF

EVERYBODY RESPONDS TO STRESS DIFFERENTLY. Some people collapse. Some give up. Some lash out. Some take charge.

While the others were crying their eyes out, the wheels were turning in Luke's head. He's the kind of person whose response to a stressful situation is to try to find a solution.

Luke assessed the situation. The TTT was gone. Mr. Maloney was gone. In a few minutes, the meeting spot would be gone. And soon after that, the whole *Titanic* would be gone, with the Flashback Four on it.

Everything would be gone. Getting back to their

own time was out of the question now.

There was only one hope for survival, and that was to get onto one of the remaining lifeboats. If they could do that, they might be rescued. They would have to start their lives all over again in 1912, of course. But at least they would live.

Maybe starting over wouldn't be so terrible, Luke thought. They would know a lot of things the people in 1912 didn't know, and that could come in handy. Plus, they still had a thousand dollars left, and that could go a long way. In any case, it was their only chance. It was either try to get on a lifeboat, or give up and go down with the ship.

"Come on, get up!" Luke commanded David, Isabel, and Julia. "Hurry! I've got a plan."

He didn't really have a plan. But he needed to motivate the others and get them out of their funk. People like it when *somebody* has a plan.

Two more distress rockets shot up in the air and exploded like Fourth of July fireworks. But none of the passengers were paying attention to them anymore. The water had already covered the meeting spot and was slowly creeping up the deck.

"How could such a tiny bump cause so much damage?" a lady commented.

It was almost two o'clock in the morning now. Time was running out and everyone was exhausted. The ship would sink in about twenty minutes. One by one, David, Isabel, and Julia pulled themselves together, got to their feet, and followed Luke.

Even now, as they ran down the deck, it still didn't *feel* like *Titanic* was sinking. The ship was so big that it felt like the water was rising *around* it, as though they were at the beach and the tide was coming in.

"Maybe they'll send some helicopters to pick up the rest of us," Julia hollered as they ran down the deck.

"Helicopters?" David yelled back. "Are you out of your mind? They didn't have helicopters in 1912!"

(True. The first practical helicopter was invented in 1939. In 1912, the *airplane* was only eight years old.)

When the Flashback Four got back to the area on the starboard side where the lifeboats were stored, they were in for a surprise. Not only were all eight lifeboats on that side of the ship full, but they were also *gone*. They could be seen in the distance, rowing away from the *Titanic*.

"What do we do *now*?" Isabel asked, stopping to catch her breath.

"We've got to go over to the other side of the ship!"

Luke hollered. "Quick! Follow me!"

After hitting a few dead ends, Luke found a narrow passageway that cut across the deck.

"I thought you said you had a plan!" David shouted as he followed Luke.

"This *is* the plan!" Luke hollered back.

"Wait up!" Isabel shouted.

Isabel and Julia were finding it hard to run in their heavy dresses, and it was even harder now that they were wet.

It was hard to run at *all*. The deck was tilted at a crazy angle. They were bumping into the walls of the passageway, running like a bunch of drunks. The water and ice covering the wood floor didn't make things easier.

Finally, they reached the other side of the ship. Fortunately, there were a few lifeboats that hadn't been launched yet.

The musicians were still out on the deck, bravely playing "Frankie and Johnny." But there was nothing they could play that was going to keep the passengers calm anymore. Order had turned into chaos. Confidence had turned into doom.

People were *everywhere*. The third-class passengers, who had been locked down in steerage while the wealthier people filled the lifeboats, had managed to break down the gates. Now they were streaming up on the deck. Large families were hauling all their worldly possessions—baby carriages, heavy wooden trunks, big suitcases. Mind you, this was long before suitcases had wheels on them. You had to *carry* them.

"Leave your things behind!" shouted a member of the crew who was loading people onto a lifeboat. "You *cannot* take any bags with you! There simply isn't enough room!"

It didn't do any good. Many of the third-class passengers were foreigners who didn't understand a word of English.

People were pushing and shoving to get close to the front of the line. Nobody was hanging back. It no longer looked safer to be on the *Titanic* than it did on a lifeboat.

"I don't think we're gonna get on," David said as the Flashback Four joined the crush of people waiting in line.

"We gotta find a way," Luke replied.

"I told you, women and children *first*!" shouted a steward at the front who seemed to be in charge of deciding who got on the lifeboat. Another steward was tearing wives away from their husbands and throwing them roughly into the boat.

"*I'm* a child!" hollered David, who was almost six feet tall and could easily be mistaken for a grown-up. He was slumping down, trying to appear a few inches shorter.

"Where are *our* lifeboats?" demanded a man carrying a big sack over his shoulder. "Where are the lifeboats reserved for the men?"

There was no need to answer him. Everybody knew there were no lifeboats reserved for the men.

The steward put two more ladies on board, and then he held up his arms and blew a whistle.

"This boat is full," he announced. "Let it go, boys!"

Some crew members turned cranks to lower the boat down to the water. The people waiting in line were furious.

"But my sister and I have been waiting here for a half an *hour*!" a lady complained.

"Sorry, ma'am," the steward explained. "The boat can only hold sixty-five people. Any more than that will swamp it."

There was no point in trying to change his mind, but people argued with him anyway. A few passengers threw their suitcases onto the lifeboat, hoping it would get them a seat. The women in the boat screamed as the suitcases landed on them.

"Dude, I can't swim," David whispered to Luke. "We gotta get on a boat."

"I'll take care of you," Luke shouted in David's ear. "I think there are more boats down this way. Come on!"

The Flashback Four ran about thirty yards up the deck until they found another lifeboat. There was room in it because some passengers had gotten out and gone back to their staterooms to get their jewelry and valuables. *Big* mistake. The staterooms were underwater at this point.

It wouldn't have mattered anyway. Stewards had gone through the ship locking the empty staterooms to prevent the third-class passengers from looting them. The people who went back for their valuables would not be on the list of survivors.

Isabel counted about a dozen seats still empty on the lifeboat. Then she counted the people in line ahead of her. It looked like the Flashback Four might possibly be able to get on.

The steward in charge of this lifeboat was fighting with a woman at the front of the line, trying to pull the suitcase out of her hands before letting her on board.

"But I need my clothes!" she screamed in a foreign accent.

He grabbed the suitcase and threw it overboard.

"*That's* what you can do with your clothes, lady!" he shouted at her as the suitcase splashed into the water below. "Go get 'em if you want 'em."

People were pushing and shoving. A baby girl was crying.

"Be patient!" one of the stewards announced. "There's plenty of room for everyone."

It was another lie too, of course. People were getting hysterical as they realized there wasn't *nearly* enough room in the lifeboat for all the passengers who were left.

People who were stuck at the back of the line began grabbing tables and chairs off the deck and throwing them overboard. They picked up anything that might float and could be used as a raft.

The line inched forward. There were only a few open seats left. Isabel prayed silently that she and her friends would get them. A man with a cane tried to muscle his way to the front of the line, as if brute force would intimidate the stewards.

"I'm a first-class passenger," he bellowed. "I paid good money for this cruise. I should be allowed on a lifeboat before the third-class people."

The steward pulled a gun out of the waistband of his pants and fired two shots in the air.

Bang! Bang!

For a moment, everybody stopped pushing and shoving.

"You put one foot on that boat and you'll be a dead man!" the steward warned the man with the cane.

"I'll be dead for sure if I stay *here*," he replied. But he backed away with his hands in the air.

Finally, the Flashback Four advanced to the front of the line.

"That's sixty-five," the steward announced. "Sorry, folks. This one's full. Lower it down, fellows."

"What?! No!"

"Oh, come on!"

"Where are we supposed to go *now*?"

David had a look of panic in his eyes. It was looking more and more like he was going to end up in the water. People were getting crazy. It seemed like there might be a riot.

"There *must* be another boat!" Luke whispered to his friends.

"What's the use?" Julia groaned. "There are too many people and not enough boats."

"*Somebody's* gonna get on them," Luke replied. "We've got as good a chance as anybody else. Come on!"

He pushed his way through the crowd, and the rest of the Flashback Four followed, looking desperately in all directions for another lifeboat.

By this time, there were a lot of men on the *Titanic* who had given up on the thought of being rescued and were resigned to their fate. There was a line of them standing at the rail, looking hopelessly at the water as their wives and children were rowed away in lifeboats. Some of them were praying or sobbing.

John Jacob Astor, one of the richest men in the world, stood next to a third-class passenger who didn't have a penny to his name. Both of them looked forlornly at the rising water. The eighteen cars that Astor owned were not going to matter now. In the end, there are some things money can't buy.

Isidor Straus, the millionaire owner of Macy's, was sitting on a deck chair holding hands with his wife, Ida. They had decided to stay together, no matter what.

A group of well-dressed men sat at a table smoking cigars and playing cards as if nothing unusual was going on around them. Their lives were essentially over and they knew it. They'd decided to go out in style. They were drowning their sorrows with alcohol.

Standing by himself, bent over with both hands on the rail, was Edward Smith, the captain of the *Titanic*. It was *his* ship. He had been in charge. There was a lot of blame to go around, but the safety of the ship, the passengers, and the crew had been his responsibility.

Smith appeared to be lost in thought, and it wasn't hard to imagine what was running through his mind: If only he hadn't ignored the multiple warnings of icebergs in the area. If only the lookouts had binoculars with them. If only he had been on the bridge when the iceberg was spotted. If only he hadn't issued the order to travel at top speed in his haste to get to New York in record time. If only he had insisted that *Titanic* carry enough lifeboats for all the passengers.

If only.

Back home in England, he had a wife and a fourteen-year-old daughter waiting for him. They would never see him again.

"There's another lifeboat!" Isabel shouted, pointing up the slanted deck. "Let's go!"

There were so many people on the port side of the ship that *Titanic* had started to lean in that direction. It looked as though it might roll over and throw off everybody who was left on it. The Flashback Four struggled to get over to the lifeboat Isabel had spotted.

"Another ship will be here to pick you up soon!" a crew member shouted through a megaphone. "For now, we need to steady the deck. All passengers please move to starboard side."

But nobody made a move to go. Word had gotten around that all the lifeboats on the starboard side were gone.

In fact, there was only one more lifeboat left on *this* side of the ship. A crowd of desperate people converged around it. It was five minutes after two o'clock now. Things were not looking good for the Flashback Four.

"Please?" a woman begged the steward who was loading the lifeboat. "I have a baby."

"There must be a hundred people here," Julia told her friends. "No way we're going to get on."

She, Isabel, and David looked at Luke, as if he would have some simple solution to get out of this predicament. As it turned out, he *did*.

"I have a plan," he whispered to Julia. "Give that guy the thousand dollars."

"What?" she replied. "Are you crazy?"

"Bribe him," Luke told her. "If you slip him the money, maybe he'll put us in front of the line."

"That's not a bad idea," said David.

"I'm not giving him the thousand dollars," Julia said. "It's all the money I have left."

"An hour ago you didn't have *any* money at *all*," Luke reminded Julia.

"But we're gonna need that money to live on after we get rescued," she argued.

"Look, we're not gonna get rescued if we don't get on a lifeboat," Luke explained. "And we're not gonna get on a lifeboat unless you bribe that guy! So give him the money, or I will."

Luke tried to grab the bills out of Julia's pocket.

"What would *he* want the money for?" Isabel asked. "He's going to go down with the ship too!"

It was a valid point. But it didn't matter whether they bribed the guy or not. Because at that moment, the *Titanic* lurched downward again. The front of the ship was totally underwater now, and the back had risen up. The enormous propellers, each of them as wide as a house, were completely out of the water.

"Grab hold of something!" Luke shouted as he slipped and fell.

The deck was almost too steep to stand on now. Rugs, chairs, and other pieces of furniture were sliding down the surface, crashing into people. Luke ducked

as a wooden crate went flying past him, nearly decapi-
tating him. A few people who hadn't been able to grab
on to a rail or something slid off the *Titanic* and into
the water.

"It's every man for himself now!" somebody
shouted.

Some people were jumping into the water, hoping
to grab on to a piece of debris floating below. Everybody was screaming.

"I can't swim!" David shouted over the noise
around him as he hung on desperately.

"This would be a great time to learn," Luke shouted
back.

"Hold on!" Isabel yelled.

"I can't look!" screamed Julia.

Using what strength he had left, Luke pulled himself along the rail until he reached the girls, who were
hanging on to a rope.

"Please don't take this the wrong way," he told
them, "but it might be a good idea to take some of
those clothes off. It's gonna be hard to swim after your
dresses get wet."

Isabel and Julia struggled to pull off their dresses.
They were down to their underwear.

Meanwhile, Luke slid down a few feet until he got

back to David, who had a terrified look in his eyes as he held on to a metal pipe.

"Okay, I need you to listen to me," Luke said as he threw off his bathrobe. "When I count to three, I need you to hold your breath and jump. Got it? I'm going to grab you as soon as you hit the water. You're gonna be okay."

"What if there are sharks down there?" David asked, scanning the water below.

"There are no sharks," Luke insisted. "Are you with me? We can do this together."

"Okay, I'm with you," David said, throwing off his bathrobe.

"Girls, are you with us?" Luke asked. "On the count of three we're gonna jump."

"Okay," shouted Isabel and Julia.

"One . . . two . . . three . . . Now *jump*!"

They jumped.

CHAPTER 13

THE SHOT

THE DECK OF THE *TITANIC* WAS A LOT LOWER than it had been an hour earlier, but it was still a long way down to the water. If you've ever jumped off a high diving board, you can imagine what it felt like. The Flashback Four screamed as they fell, flailing their arms and legs in the air.

David held his breath and closed his eyes tightly. He hit the surface butt-first, making the biggest splash of the four. The cold water was a shock to the system, but he was so afraid of drowning that he didn't even notice the temperature at first. David was sure he would immediately sink to the bottom of the ocean like a stone, but of course he naturally bobbed right back up to the surface.

Luke held the camera up in the air as he fell. He was determined to keep it dry. Somehow, he managed to swim over to David and hold him afloat with one hand. Isabel and Julia, who had both competed on swim teams when they were younger, paddled over to help out.

"Help!" David shouted. "I can't swim!"

"We've got you," Julia assured him, taking one arm. "Relax! Stop kicking! You're stiff as a board!"

"It's *cold*!" Isabel yelled.

It was indeed *very* cold, close to freezing. They could see the breath coming out of their mouths. But for the moment, keeping David's head above the water was the bigger issue. Luke handed the camera to Isabel so he could take care of David on his own.

There was really no good reason to protect the camera anymore. Digital photography would not be around for another eighty years, so Luke would not be able to do anything with the pictures. But he was an optimist. He *still* thought there might be some way to get back to his own time, as unlikely as that might be.

"I got you, dude," Luke told David.

Treading water, he wrapped an arm around David's chest and held on to him from behind, the way he had been taught in his lifesaving course. It didn't seem possible for Luke to keep David—a *big* guy—afloat. But somehow, when life is on the line, you call up a hidden reserve of untapped strength. You don't feel the cold. You can lift things you never lifted before. You can hold your breath longer than is humanly possible. It's sort of like having temporary superpowers.

When David realized he was in good hands and he wasn't going to sink, he calmed down a little.

"You sure you got me?" he asked.

"Trust me," Luke replied.

But Luke knew he couldn't keep both of them afloat indefinitely. His toes and fingertips were already getting numb.

"I think I see something!" Isabel said excitedly. "Over there. Isn't that a lifeboat?"

It was. Sixteen lifeboats were bobbing in the water around the sinking *Titanic*, and several of them were within swimming distance.

"Okay," Luke told David, "I need to let go of you now so you can swim to that lifeboat over there."

"What?! I can't swim!" David shouted, immediately tensing up. "Don't let go!"

"You *can*, dude," Luke said calmly. "You've got to trust me on this."

"I'm gonna drown," David yelled, grabbing on to Luke. "As soon as you let go of me, I'm gonna go under!"

"You're *not* gonna go under," Julia told him. "Your body wants to float. It doesn't want to sink."

"How do *you* know what my body wants to do?" David shouted at her.

"Listen to me," Luke calmly told his friend. "I need you to tread water—nice and easy—just move your arms and your legs slowly, like this. Okay? You can do it!"

"It's easy," Isabel assured David. "See? Any five-year-old kid can do it."

"I'm not a five-year-old kid!" David hollered.

"Smooth and easy," Luke said, relaxing his grip on David. "You don't need to flail around to stay afloat. That'll just tire you out. Calm down. Fill your lungs with air. They're like balloons inside your body. They help you float."

Luke let go. There was a look of terrified panic on David's face, but he did what he was told. He took a deep breath and moved his arms and legs rhythmically. When he saw that his head was staying above the surface, a little smile appeared on David's face.

"See? You're treading water!" Isabel told him.

"The movement helps keep you warm too," added Julia.

"Okay, you're doing great, David," Luke said. "Now we need you to paddle in this direction. Over here. Can you do that?"

"Like this?" David asked, as he did a simple doggie paddle.

"Just like that," Luke told him. "Follow me."

As David inched forward with Luke in front of him, Isabel and Julia swam ahead to catch up with the lifeboat, maybe forty feet away.

The boat was about three-quarters full. There was certainly room for the Flashback Four, and a few more people as well. But whoever was rowing the boat was making no effort to rescue them. If anything, the boat seemed to be moving away from them.

But Isabel and Julia caught up with it and hoisted themselves on board. Nobody reached out a hand to help them in, or even made eye contact with them. The women and children on the lifeboat just sat there in shocked silence, shivering and whimpering, wrapped in blankets to stay warm.

There was just one man on the lifeboat—a big guy who called himself Mr. Strong. Each boat had been assigned a crew member to do the rowing. The women—of course—were considered too weak and ladylike to row a boat themselves. It wasn't clear if the guy's last name was Strong, or he just *called* himself Strong because he wanted to seem tough.

In the water, Luke was urging David on as he dog-paddled toward the lifeboat.

"You're doing great!" Luke shouted. "Keep going!"

David was panting and gasping for breath, exhausted. He was in good shape from playing basketball and football, but he had never done anything as strenuous as this. Luke grabbed him and pulled him along for the last few yards to the boat. The girls reached out and hoisted David on board, like they had caught a big fish. Luke tumbled into the boat right after him.

"We *made* it," he said to his friend. "I told you we'd make it."

"Thanks, man," David said, his chest heaving. "You saved my life."

"Don't mention it," Luke told him. "And no charge for the swimming lesson, by the way."

Mr. Strong turned around and saw he had four more passengers huddling together in the back of the boat. He had a scowl on his face.

"That's *all*," he grumbled. "Nobody else. Take your seats and keep your mouths shut and we'll all get along."

The Flashback Four looked at each other.

"What is *his* problem?" Julia whispered.

"Looks like that guy's having a *bad* day," whispered David, causing the others to giggle quietly. David had recovered enough from his swimming ordeal to be cracking jokes.

Mr. Strong began to row hard, as if he was in a race.

"Excuse me, sir," Isabel said. "Do you mind my asking why you're working so hard? We're in the middle of the ocean."

"Yeah, where are you rowing to?" asked an older woman. "Why don't we just wait here for another ship to come and rescue us?"

Mr. Strong stopped rowing for a moment and turned around. He was breathing heavily, panting and sweating. Rowing a heavy wooden boat with sixty people in it is not easy.

"You see that?" he said, pointing to the *Titanic*, about fifty yards away. "When she goes under, there's gonna be a big suction all around her. If we're anywhere close to her, she's gonna take us down with her. The farther we get away, the better."

"Let us help," Luke offered. "My friends and I can row."

"No!" Mr. Strong barked as he started rowing again. "This is a *man's* job. You just sit there and be quiet."

The Flashback Four turned around to look at the *Titanic*. It was slanted down, almost like a wounded animal. The lights of the ship were still on, miraculously. The other lifeboats were floating around it. The water was very calm, like glass. There was something beautiful about the scene.

At the same time, of course, it was a very sad sight. They were close enough to see many people still on board, hanging on for dear life.

Isabel handed Luke the camera, which she had been keeping dry ever since they jumped into the water.

"Here," she whispered. "You might as well take the picture. This is something you don't see every day."

Luke held the camera low so the other people on the lifeboat couldn't see it, but nobody was paying attention to him anyway. They were all staring at the *Titanic*.

"Why bother taking the picture?" asked Julia.

"Why not?" said David. "What have we got to lose?"

Luke shrugged and pushed the On button. The

screen on the back of the camera lit up. He pointed it at the *Titanic* and framed the shot carefully, so the ship filled the little screen with a few lifeboats floating in front of it. Then he pushed the shutter release.

It was perfect. He didn't even have to take a second shot.

"That's it," Luke whispered when the image appeared on the screen. "That's why we came here. This is the picture that Miss Z told us to shoot."

He passed the camera around for the others to admire.

"Too bad she'll never see it," said Isabel. "Too bad *nobody* will ever see it, except us."

Mr. Strong kept rowing away from the *Titanic*. Everybody else in the boat was still staring at it. You couldn't take your eyes off it. The ship looked even *bigger* when viewed from a distance. The bow was completely underwater, the stern out of it.

There was a sudden *boom*, and sparks shot out a funnel. One of the boilers must have exploded when the seawater flooded in.

It was eighteen minutes after two. You could see the ship tilting now and hear the awful sounds as it moved—popping, cracking, crashing, breaking glass. Sound gets amplified when water cools the air above it and slows down the sound waves. People in the lifeboats could hear every bang, every call for help.

Suddenly all the lights on the *Titanic* went out. Then they flashed on again for just an instant, and then went out for good. Only the faint outline of the ship could be seen in the dark now.

Next came the roar. It was a horrifying, other-worldly rumbling sound as the weight of the tilting engines and boilers caused them to break loose from their moorings and slide along the bottom of the ship, smashing into each other.

"Oh my God!" exclaimed one of the women on the lifeboat.

"No!" groaned another. Some women just covered their mouths with their hands, speechless. Even Mr.

Strong stopped rowing for a moment to watch with wonder.

Titanic was at a forty-five-degree angle now. The forward funnel broke off and tumbled down, hitting the water with a loud *slap* and almost landing on top of a lifeboat. Sparks shot out of the funnel and sizzled when they hit the water.

The weight of the three enormous propellers was just too much at that angle for the *Titanic* to hold together. There was a terrifying crunching sound of bending steel and iron as the ship broke in two pieces, almost right down the middle. The front end filled with water and snapped away like a twig, disappearing beneath the surface.

Free from the weight of the bow, the stern of *Titanic* rose so it was standing straight up. It looked like a duck that had dipped its beak into the water. For a minute or two the *Titanic* just sat there like that, as if it couldn't decide what to do next. But the stern was filling up with water too.

It was twenty minutes after two o'clock in the morning.

And then, the whole thing slid down. There was no suction, as Mr. Strong had predicted. There was barely a ripple on the water. The only noise was the collective gasp on the lifeboat as the great ship slipped straight down. It was like the ocean took a mighty gulp and swallowed it.

The unsinkable *Titanic* was gone.

CHAPTER 14

THE DEAD AND DYING

BACK IN BOSTON, MISS Z WAS FRANTICALLY TAP-
ping keys and fumbling with her computer. Droplets of
sweat had appeared on her forehead.

"Why did Isabel stop responding to my texts?" she
said to Mrs. Vader, who was looking over her shoulder
at the screen. "They were supposed to go to the meeting spot so I could pick them up. Where is she?"

There had been a horrible mistake, and Miss Z did
not tolerate mistakes—by herself or by others. She
thought she had carefully prepared for every possible
circumstance. But she hadn't anticipated this last-
minute glitch. She was frustrated.

In her mind, Miss Z imagined the Flashback Four
being swept off the *Titanic* by a big wave and thrown

into the sea, like so many others who lost their lives on that horrible night.

She thought, what if she couldn't retrieve the kids? How would she explain to their parents what had happened to them? There would be lawsuits, for sure. Multimillion dollar lawsuits. As much money as she had, this could bankrupt her. Her reputation would be shot. The police would get involved. She could go to jail.

Miss Z wiped her face with a tissue. All the money in the world couldn't help her get out of this mess, just as it couldn't help John Jacob Astor or his wealthy friends on the *Titanic*.

She and Astor probably had the same thought going through their minds—maybe technology *isn't* the answer to every problem. Maybe mother nature is more powerful than anything we can build.

Miss Z was suddenly questioning things she had never questioned before. Maybe she should have never invested so much time and money into the Board. Maybe she should never have allowed the kids to choose a meeting spot at the front of the ship— the part that would be underwater first. Maybe she shouldn't have sent children on this mission in the first place—just to get a photograph to add to her collection. It was too much responsibility for kids. And she never even *got* the photo! She wiped her face again, cursing herself.

Then there was the other little problem Miss Z had to deal with. Still standing in front of the Board was Mr. Maloney, the *Titanic* deckhand whom she had accidentally summoned into the future. What was she going to do about *him*?

Where would he sleep that night? How would she explain him to the police? He stood there, still unclear where he was or how he got there.

"Uh, can I go home now?" he asked timidly.

"No!" Miss Z barked, barely looking up from her computer screen.

"Something must have gone wrong," said Mrs. Vader, trying to be helpful.

"Well, of *course* something went wrong!" Miss Z snapped back. "The question is, *what* went wrong, and how can we fix it?"

Neither of them had any way of knowing that the TTT had slipped out of Isabel's hand as she fell on the deck of the *Titanic*, and it was now at the bottom of the ocean. They also had no idea that the Flashback Four were sitting in a lifeboat floating about a quarter mile from where the *Titanic* used to be.

She racked her brains to come up with a solution. By now, the meeting spot was probably underwater. How could she bring back the Flashback Four? The Board was an amazing piece of technology in being able to send human beings through time, but it did not have the capability to *find* human beings who were lost. She tried anyway, clicking everything on the screen, even things she knew wouldn't work.

"It's not working!" she said, frustrated. "Why isn't it working?"

"Maybe you oughta send 'em a telegram," suggested Mr. Maloney.

"Shut up!" barked Miss Z.

In the second or two after the *Titanic* slipped under the surface, it was strangely quiet and peaceful on the ocean. The mirror image of the stars hanging in the sky was reflected in the water. A light gray, smoky vapor hung over the surface. It was all that could be seen in the inky darkness.

In the lifeboat, bobbing up and down gently, were the Flashback Four. Shivering and groaning quietly in the dark, all the kids were filled with fear of the unknown, wondering what would happen next.

At least he'd taken the picture, Luke thought. Even though he had no way to deliver it to Miss Z, he had completed the mission. That counted for something.

The other passengers in the lifeboat just stared at the spot where the *Titanic* had been visible moments earlier, as if it was going to resurface like a whale and continue on its way. It didn't seem possible that an object so large could even *fit* inside the ocean. Some of the people in the lifeboat felt guilty for having survived while so many others had perished. And some just sobbed.

After a few moments of silence, after the survivors had the chance to digest what they had just witnessed, they became aware of a horrible sound—screaming. The water was filled with people shouting, gasping, thrashing in desperation to keep their heads above the surface. There were hundreds of them. Maybe a thousand or more. All kinds of junk was floating around, some of it tied together to form makeshift rafts. People were clinging to crates, chairs, planks, anything that would float.

Mr. Strong stopped rowing and turned around to watch the spectacle. But he seemed more concerned when he noticed that his shoes were wet.

"The blasted boat is filling up with water!" he shouted, throwing in a few curse words to show his displeasure.

Indeed it was. There was a two-inch circular hole at the bottom of the lifeboat. In fact, there was a hole like that at the bottom of *every* lifeboat. The holes had been put there intentionally so that when the boat was sitting on the deck of the Titanic, rainwater wouldn't pool up at the bottom. Somebody was supposed to plug the hole before lowering a lifeboat into the water. That somebody would have been Mr. Strong. But in his haste to launch the boat, he'd forgotten.

"Where's the blasted plug?" he shouted, as if any of the passengers could help, or even knew what he was talking about. He got down on his hands and knees until he found the plug and managed to jam it in the hole.

"Start bailing!" he ordered. "We need to get rid of this water."

"Where is the bucket?" one of the ladies asked.

"We ain't got no bloomin' bucket!" Mr. Strong shouted at her. "Use your hat, lady! It ain't doing no good up on your head!"

"There's no need to be rude, young man," she replied as she took off her hat and started bailing out the water with it. A few other women did the same. The Flashback Four joined in to help, bailing out water with their hands. It took a few minutes to empty out the bottom of the boat.

"My feet are cold and soaking wet," an older lady complained.

"Shut your yap!" Mr. Strong barked at her. "You're lucky to be alive."

"The same could be said of *you*, young man!" the old lady said. "Why are you here anyway? I thought these boats were reserved for the women and children."

"*Somebody* has to row this thing," Mr. Strong mumbled.

"I don't see you rowing," another lady said. "You'll have some explaining to do when we get rescued."

"That's *if* we get rescued," somebody at the other side of the boat added.

It was a big if. The people in the lifeboats had no expectation, no assurance that they would ever be rescued. For all they knew, the nearest ship was hundreds of miles away. They could be floating there for many days. There was no food or drinking water in the boat. And even though the ocean was calm, a wave could come along at any time and easily flip over a lifeboat.

Their teeth chattering, the shivering Flashback Four huddled close together under a blanket for warmth. David's fingers had gone numb. Isabel's and Julia's long hair was frozen solid into stiff clumps.

"I'm *soooo* cold," Julia groaned.

"Imagine how cold the people out *there* feel," said Luke, pointing at the sea of men, women, and children bobbing in the distance.

Few of the desperate swimmers had probably ever heard of *hypothermia*, but that's what they were experiencing. The water temperature was below freezing and body heat is lost more quickly in water. If your core body temperature dips below ninety-five degrees, that's the definition of hypothermia.

Shivering is the first symptom. After that, a person's heart rate and breathing get faster. They become pale and have trouble moving their muscles. If they don't warm up, their lips, ears, fingers, and toes turn blue. They can't speak or think clearly. Then their pulse gets slow, and they become sleepy and confused. They may have hallucinations. Finally, they stop breathing and their heart stops.

Some of the people in the water were already dead. Some were dying. Everyone else was struggling. Their voices carried across the water.

"Boat ahoy!"

"Room for one more in a boat?"

"Help!"

Isabel stood up so she could look around and count the people on the lifeboat. It was hard to see them all, but she guessed there were about sixty. That meant there was room for at least five more.

"We should go back and rescue some of those people," she said to the group, but directed her words at Mr. Strong. "There's room for five or six more on this boat."

"Ain't gonna happen," Mr. Strong barked. "We take one of 'em and all the rest of 'em will wanna climb aboard. That'll swamp the boat and we *all* die. Is that what you want?"

It was a fair point, but Isabel couldn't bear to just sit there and do nothing while people in the water were fighting for their lives.

"I say we put it to a vote," she suggested.

"Take all the votes you want," said Mr. Strong. "I'm not going back there."

"All those in favor of going back to rescue some people, say aye."

"Aye," said all the members of the Flashback Four.

"All those opposed, say nay," said Mr. Strong.

"Nay," came a chorus of voices.

"See? I told you so," he said.

"But people are *dying* out there!" Isabel begged.

"Sea travel is risky business," Mr. Strong told her. "They knew what they was gettin' into. I'm not here to worry about the dead. I'm here to take care of the living."

"How will you people sleep at night?" Isabel shouted at the ladies before sitting back down, disgusted.

"Cut them a break," David whispered to her. "They lost their husbands. They lost their fathers."

"All the more reason why . . ."

There was no point in arguing. It didn't matter anyway, because during the discussion a man in the water had somehow managed to swim over and grab hold of the side of the lifeboat. He didn't have a life jacket on. There was a pleading look in his eyes as he tried to climb aboard.

"Save one life!" he begged. "Please . . ."

When Mr. Strong saw the struggling man, he lifted one oar out of the water and almost casually poked the guy in the head with it. He screamed in pain, let go, and slipped under the surface.

"No!" Isabel shouted.

David and Luke looked at each other. Both of them

had seen some pretty bad stuff in the rough neighbor-hoods of Boston, but neither of them had ever seen anything as cruel as that. No words had to be spoken. The boys got up from their seats and went over to Mr. Strong, who had his hands on both oars.

"Sit down!" Mr. Strong shouted at them. "You'll capsize us. I'm in charge here. You listen to what I say."

David and Luke grabbed him around the neck and together they yanked him backward off the seat and threw him roughly to the floor of the boat. Julia and Isabel grabbed for the oars before they could fall into the water.

"Shut up!" Luke shouted at Mr. Strong. "This is a mutiny. *We're* in charge of the boat now."

"Keep your mouth shut or we'll throw you over-board," David added.

Mr. Strong was shocked and speechless. No child had ever spoken to him like that. He looked up at the ladies on the boat, as if one of them would rise to his defense. None of them did. They looked frightened. It didn't seem to matter to them who was in charge, as long as *somebody* was in charge.

"You heard him," said Julia. "Keep your mouth shut or we'll throw you overboard."

David and Luke took Mr. Strong's seat and each

grabbed an oar. They were big and heavy, but with a good deal of effort, the boys managed to turn the boat around and head back toward the spot where *Titanic* had gone under. Mr. Strong sat there sullenly.

"Over there!" Julia said, pointing ahead. "I think I heard voices coming from over there."

It took about fifteen minutes to reach the spot. The cries for help could still be heard, but they were growing fewer and fainter with each passing minute.

When they finally got to where Julia had pointed, they were confronted by a sight that nobody should ever have to see—hundreds of lifeless bodies floating in the water.

Most of them were men, but there were some women and children too. Luke leaned over to grab one of them by the life jacket and turn it over to see if the person might still be alive. He wasn't. It looked like he was sleeping, but he was dead. One of the ladies in the boat vomited.

There was nobody left alive to rescue.

STAYING ALIVE

"LET'S GET OUT OF HERE," ISABEL SAID SOFTLY.

Luke and David turned the boat around slowly, being careful not to touch any of the floating bodies with the oars.

"See? I *told* you not to go back," grumbled Mr. Strong.

The women in the lifeboat had been quiet up until now. Most of them were from the upper classes and hadn't encountered much adversity in their lives. They were still in a state of shock. It was impossible for them to comprehend that the *Titanic* had disappeared, and now—less than a half an hour later—most of the passengers were dead. Hypothermia works fast.

Nobody wants to believe their loved one is gone. The women on the boat held out hope that their husbands, brothers, and fathers might possibly have found seats in other lifeboats. A chorus of their voices began calling out.

"Thomas! Can you hear me, Thomas?"

"Is there a William Johnson in your boat?"

"We have no men in our boat at all," came a reply.

Mr. Strong sat in the corner, sulking.

Except for the stars dotting the sky, it was pitch dark. That's when the eyes can play tricks on you. In the distance, a small white light appeared to flicker for a moment.

"Did you see that?" somebody asked.

"It was a light," another passenger said. "I saw it too."

"Is that a ship?" one of the ladies asked.

"Where?"

"Over there!"

"We're going to be rescued!"

There was a brief celebration. Everyone stared at the spot where the dot of light had appeared, but it didn't appear again. Hope quickly faded.

"Maybe it was just a mirage," Julia guessed.

"I think mirages only happen in the desert," said Isabel.

The survivors in the lifeboats were beginning to worry about their *own* survival now. They didn't know whether or not a rescue ship was coming to pick them up. The Flashback Four didn't know what might happen next either. They never thought it would come to this.

"Move over," one of the ladies said to the woman sitting next to her. "You're taking up the whole seat."

"*You* move over," the second lady said. "I was here first."

"But I was in first class," the first lady replied.

Luke stood up to face the two ladies.

"Knock it off!" he shouted at them. "You're both alive! Be thankful for that!"

"There are no classes here," David added. "We're all together now."

It was quiet for a minute while everyone calmed down.

"He's right," one of the other women said. "We're all together here."

"Perhaps we should say a prayer," a lady in the back suggested.

"I am Episcopalian," said a voice in the back.

"I'm a Methodist," said another.

"I am a Lutheran," somebody on the left side of the boat said.

"I'm Jewish," said somebody on the right.

It seemed like a problem. Isabel interrupted the

silence by starting to recite the only prayer she remembered by heart. One by one, other people in the boat joined in . . .

"Our Father, which art in heaven,
Hallowed be thy Name.
Thy Kingdom come.
Thy will be done in earth,
As it is in heaven.
Give us this day our daily bread.
And forgive us our trespasses,
As we forgive them that trespass against us.
And lead us not into temptation,
But deliver us from evil.
For thine is the kingdom,
The power, and the glory,
For ever and ever."

"Amen," mumbled a chorus of voices.

"I don't believe in *any* religion," said a lady in the back of the boat when they were finished. "Not anymore. How could a loving and all-powerful God allow tragedy like this to happen?"

"God works in mysterious ways," another lady replied.

"Let's not get started," somebody else said.

They sat there in the darkness for what seemed like a long time. Luke was restless. He didn't like waiting in line for Red Sox tickets, or waiting in line for the cannolis at Mike's Pastry in Boston. And he certainly didn't like waiting for a ship to come and save his life.

"We've got to *do* something," Luke said. "If a ship came to rescue us, how would it even know we're here?"

"The boy is right," one of the ladies said. "We're invisible in the dark. A ship coming to rescue us might run right over us."

"We should make a signal," suggested Isabel. "Does anybody have a cigarette lighter?"

"I have a box of matches," one lady volunteered.

"I have some paper," offered another. "It's pretty dry."

"You can burn my hat," someone else said.

They passed the matches and hat forward. David put the hat at the end of his oar and lit one of the feathers. It flared up. Once a little fire was established, Luke and David held the oar high in the air so it could be seen from a distance.

"You're wastin' your time, I say," said Mr. Strong.

"Ain't nobody out there to see that."

"We've got to try *something*," said Julia.

Actually, Mr. Strong was right. There was no ship in the area to see the burning hat. But people in the other lifeboats saw it. Soon there were hats, handkerchiefs, newspapers, and other objects in flames lighting up the night. A green flare shot up from one lifeboat.

In a few minutes, the fires had burned out in all the boats and the only light that could be seen was a wooden cane with a little flashlight at the end that somebody was waving in the air. A feeling of gloom settled over the passengers.

"Happy now?" Mr. Strong grumbled. "You coulda set the whole boat on fire."

The Flashback Four were pretty sure all the people who made it into the *Titanic*'s lifeboats *did* get rescued. But they didn't know for sure, and they didn't know how long it took. None of them had researched that part of the story.

"We'll be rescued soon, I'm sure of it," one lady said. "Keep a positive outlook! That's what I say."

"*You* keep a positive outlook," said another one. "My husband is dead. I have nothing." Then she started weeping.

All was silent as the women in the boat thought

about the loved ones they had lost. Luke, David, Julia, and Isabel kept quiet, out of respect.

"I'm hungry," somebody finally said.

"I'm thirsty."

Everyone searched their pockets, but nobody in the boat had thought to bring anything to eat. And in 1912, people didn't carry bottles of water with them wherever they went.

It's commonly known that a person can survive a few weeks without food. But water is another thing. Most of the human body is made of it, and every living cell needs it to keep functioning. It lubricates our joints, regulates our body temperature, and helps to flush waste from our system. You can't live for more than a few days without water.

Isabel looked around. There was nothing but water for hundreds of miles in every direction. But you can't drink *salt* water. It reminded her of a poem she had learned in her honors English class . . .

"Water, water, everywhere,
And all the boards did shrink;
Water, water, everywhere,
Nor any drop to drink."

"What's that?" asked Julia.

"'The Rime of the Ancient Mariner,'" Isabel told her. "It's by Samuel Taylor Coleridge. We had to memorize it in school."

"Never heard of it," said Julia.

It was past three o'clock in the morning now. Everybody was cold and wet. Hungry and thirsty. Frustrated. Angry. Worried. Sorrowful.

But most of all, they were tired. Few people in the lifeboat could remember the last time they had slept.

And so, one by one, they fell asleep.

CHAPTER 16

A BEAUTIFUL MORNING

WHILE THE FLASHBACK FOUR AND THE OTHERS IN the lifeboat slept fitfully, the Earth kept right on spinning. As it did, the stars gradually disappeared, and the sun crept up over the horizon. The sky was turning light blue, and the temperature was on the way up.

When the survivors of the *Titanic* woke up, they were treated to an amazing sight—a string of icebergs stretching out in all directions. Some of them towered sixty feet above the water. Others—called *growlers*— were the size of small cars. The morning sun reflecting off the ice made it sparkle with color—pink, blue, lavender, and white.

It was a beautiful scene, or it *would* have been a beautiful scene if you didn't stop and remember that a berg just like one of those had sliced open the *Titanic* and caused the death of so many innocent people.

"I thought maybe it was all a dream," Julia said after she opened her eyes. "But it really happened."

Julia's hair was all messed up. *Everyone's* hair was messed up, their clothes wrinkled and stained. The society ladies who spent hours every day making themselves look pretty now looked, well, pretty lousy. It's hard to look perfect when you've spent the night sleeping while sitting up in your clothes. And nobody cared. They were all in the same boat (so to speak). The important thing was that they had survived the night.

The water was no longer as calm as it had been the night before. Ocean swells lifted the boat up and lowered it down again. A few people on one side got up and moved to the other side to help balance the weight. Nobody needed to be told. They just did it because it had to be done. In the distance, the people in some of the other lifeboats had tied their boats together in a little flotilla.

As the ladies were stretching their arms and saying "Good morning" to one another, there was a very faint sound in the distance. It might have been a foghorn or a bird. Or it could have been just wishful thinking.

Nobody got excited until an object could be clearly seen on the horizon. It wasn't a mirage, and it wasn't a hallucination.

"I see a ship!" somebody shouted. "A big one!"

"We're going to be saved!"

The yelling and cheering that erupted was so loud that it overwhelmed another sound—the blast of the ship's whistle. Women who had been total strangers a few hours earlier were hugging each other like long-lost friends. They almost tipped the boat over in their exuberance. It would be hard to imagine happier people than these.

It was sort of like the old joke:

Q: Why are you banging your head against the wall?

A: Because it feels so good when I stop.

"Over here!" Everyone was shouting and waving their hands in the air.

While several ships had received the SOS from *Titanic* before it went under, only one had come to its rescue. That was the *Carpathia*, a nine-year-old passenger steamship that was heading for Europe. When the captain learned that *Titanic* was in trouble, he quickly changed course and rushed to help.

Carpathia was about half the size of *Titanic* and

couldn't move as fast. The captain had the ship's hot water turned off so he could push its engines up to twenty miles per hour. *Carpathia* had come from fifty-eight miles away, weaving its way carefully around the icebergs dotting the north Atlantic.

"Let's go!" David shouted to Luke as the rescue ship got closer. "Row!"

The pair pulled the oars with renewed enthusiasm, and as a result their lifeboat was one of the first ones to reach the *Carpathia*.

As it got closer, the engines were cut to reduce the wake and avoid bumping into any of the lifeboats.

"Ahoy!" a crew member shouted from the deck. "Are you people from the *Titanic*?"

It seemed like the dumbest question in history.

Why *else* would they be floating around the middle of the Atlantic Ocean in a lifeboat?

"Yes!" everyone shouted.

"And we are more than a little happy to see you!" one of the ladies hollered.

A series of slings and rope ladders were lowered along the side of the *Carpathia*. Luke and David maneuvered the lifeboat over. Julia grabbed a rope and tied it to the lifeboat.

"Age before beauty," Isabel said as she helped an elderly lady stand up and get into a rope sling. "Okay, take her up!"

The crew of the *Carpathia* pulled the sling up using a pulley system, and then lowered it back down to pick up the next passenger.

The Flashback Four helped the rest of the ladies step out of the boat. It took a while to get all of them. Some of the ladies were very old, and some of them were injured or unsteady on their feet.

Eventually, the only people left in the lifeboat were the Flashback Four and Mr. Strong.

"After you, sir," David said, bowing deeply and gesturing for Mr. Strong to get into the sling.

Mr. Strong grunted and got in.

Finally, Isabel and Julia hopped into two slings,

which bumped against the side of the *Carpathia* a few times on the way up. Neither of the girls seemed to mind. Luke and David decided to race up the rope ladders instead of waiting for the slings to be lowered back down again.

It took a few hours to pick up all the passengers in the lifeboats. By eight thirty in the morning, the seven hundred survivors of the *Titanic* were safely aboard the *Carpathia*. As they got up to the top, many people fell to their knees and kissed the deck as if it was solid ground. Luke, David, Julia, and Isabel had a long group hug.

"We made it," Julia said, tears streaming down her cheeks.

Nobody seemed to be bothered that the Flashback Four were standing there in their underwear. The deck was littered with *Titanic* survivors milling around in various stages of undress.

You have to hand it to the passengers and crew of the *Carpathia*. They could have been annoyed that their trip had been interrupted. They would have had every right to be angry when word got around that the captain had decided to change course and go back to New York instead of continuing on to Europe. Instead, they welcomed the *Titanic* survivors, giving them everything from hot soup, coffee, and tea to new shoes and toothbrushes.

"You poor dears," a woman with an Italian accent said, putting an arm around Julia. "What you must have been through!"

"You don't know the half of it," Julia replied.

The Italian woman insisted on taking the Flashback Four to her stateroom and giving them clothes to wear. She said she had eight children, so she had things in lots of different sizes. Isabel and Julia had fun pulling dresses out of the trunk on the floor. They were nowhere near as fancy as the clothes they had been wearing before, but they were perfectly nice.

"My kids will never miss them," she said as Luke found a pair of shoes that almost fit his big feet. The Flashback Four thanked her repeatedly, and Julia tried to give her a wet hundred-dollar bill, but she refused to accept it.

"Do unto others as you would have them do unto you," the Italian lady said. "That's the Golden Rule."

It was past nine o'clock in the morning. The blast of a horn and the vibration under the floor indicated that the *Carpathia*'s engines had started up again. By the time the Flashback Four had changed into their new clothes and got back up to the deck, the ship was already churning through the water.

The rail at the stern of the ship was lined with *Titanic* survivors looking sadly into the distance. So many of their loved ones were gone. Later, the *Carpathia* would come to be referred to as "the ship of widows."

The Flashback Four went to the rail too. It was impossible not to glance backward, to where the *Titanic* had been floating a few hours earlier.

"Do you think there's anything we could have done?" David asked wistfully.

"We tried," Isabel replied. "We did what we could."

They walked up the deck to the front of the ship, where some of the other passengers had gathered.

"What happens now?" asked Julia, looking at the distant horizon as *Carpathia* sliced through the water.

It was a good question. None of them had spent any time researching what happened *after* the *Titanic* sank. They assumed they would be safe at home by that time, and it wouldn't matter.

"I don't know," said David. "I guess our lives begin all over again."

THE FUTURE

STARTING OVER.

It sounds like it could be a *good* thing to go back and live your life all over again in a different time and a different place. You'd get a fresh start. Everything would be new, different, and exciting. All the dumb things you did or said in the past would be forgotten. The people you don't like would be gone. And of course, you would know more than everybody else, because you would have lived through things that hadn't happened yet.

The first thing that Luke thought about was his beloved Boston Red Sox. It was April, the beginning of baseball season. He knew the Sox would have a great season and win the World Series in 1912. And just two years later, they would sign a teenage pitcher who would lead the team to *three* World Series championships and change the game of baseball forever. His name was Babe Ruth. What a great time to be a Red Sox fan! Maybe starting over again in 1912 wouldn't be so bad.

David wasn't having such pleasant thoughts. He was thinking about the things his parents had told him that African Americans had to deal with every day back in "the good old days." Bigotry. Prejudice. Discrimination. Hotels, restaurants, and water fountains you weren't allowed to use because of your skin color.

And the Red Sox, of course. They would be the *last* team in major league baseball to put a black player on the field. He would have to wait until 1959—a dozen years after Jackie Robinson broke the color barrier—before the Sox would finally sign infielder Pumpsie Green.

David also remembered from his social studies class that World War I would start in 1914 and last four years. He would be eighteen when the war ended. He might very well get drafted and sent to fight and possibly die.

Like David, Isabel was filled with dread about starting over in 1912. She would have to spend the rest of her life without her parents. She wouldn't have her brothers and sister anymore. Her grandparents would be gone. So would her other friends back home. She would never see her house again, or her bedroom with her stuffed animals in it. She would never see her school, or her teachers. Everything she knew and loved would be gone. She would miss her kitten, Foozle.

Isabel did the math in her head. Her parents were born in the 1970s. So if she was starting all over again in 1912, she would be in her *seventies* around the time when her parents would be born. She could meet them possibly, but then she would be meeting them when they were just kids, and that would be weird. The thought of living the rest of her life without her loved ones made her want to cry again.

"I have no family anymore," Isabel told the others.

They gathered around, putting their arms around her.

"We'll be your family," Julia told her.

For Julia, starting life over again in 1912 presented all kinds of interesting opportunities. She still had those ten hundred-dollar bills in her pocket. That was more than the average American worker made all *year* in 1912. You could buy sugar for four cents a pound and a dozen eggs for fourteen cents. They could live like royalty on that money.

Not only that, but it occurred to Julia that there was a way she could make much *more* money than that.

"Hey, guys," she said as they walked the deck of the *Carpathia*. "I just got a *brilliant* idea!"

"This I want to hear," David said.

Julia lowered her voice so the people walking around could not hear her.

"We could make a fortune by inventing something nobody ever heard of," she whispered.

"What do you mean?" Isabel asked.

"It's 1912," Julia explained. "There's a lot of stuff we grew up with that they don't have here. We can invent it, sell it, and make a killing."

"Like what?" asked Luke.

"Like . . . television," Julia replied. "These people have no idea what television is. They've never seen one."

"So *you're* going to invent television?" asked Isabel.

"*You* know how to build a TV?"

"Well, that was a bad example," Julia said. "But there's lots of stuff that we *could* make."

As a group, they brainstormed to come up with products that people didn't have in 1912. The refrigerator (1913). The traffic light (1914). Scotch tape (1930). Twinkies (1930).

"This whole idea sounds kinda wrong," Isabel pointed out. "It's like, cheating."

"So what?" Julia said. "Nobody would ever know we came from the future. This is a survival situation, y'know. We have no parents. No homes. No nothing. All we have is what's in our heads. We've got to use our heads to survive."

A newspaper was sitting on an empty deck chair, so Julia picked it up and paged through it, looking for ideas.

"Look at this," she said. "There's no crossword puzzle in this paper. Maybe they didn't have crossword puzzles in 1912. So we could invent it!"

(Actually, the first crossword puzzles would appear just one year later, in the *New York World* newspaper.)

"Making a crossword puzzle is *hard*," Isabel said. "I saw something on TV once about the people who make crossword puzzles. They're, like, geniuses."

Julia put the newspaper back on the deck chair and kept trying to think of something they could invent that didn't exist in 1912. Luke said he had to use the bathroom, and he went off to find one. That's when Julia came up with another idea.

"I've *got* it!" she said, snapping her fingers. "The zipper!"

"Oh come on," Isabel said. "Now you're just being ridiculous."

"No, listen!" Julia said excitedly. "Remember Miss Z told us that pants didn't have zippers in 1912? We could invent the first zipper! Soon they'll be putting them on pants, jackets, backpacks, suitcases, *everything*! We'll make a fortune, you guys!"

In fact, Julia was absolutely right. While the first primitive zipper was invented long before 1912, the modern zipper was perfected by a Swedish American engineer named Gideon Sundback in December of 1913. He patented it in 1917. It wasn't called a zipper until 1923.

"So your brilliant plan is for us to invent the zipper?" David asked.

"Yeah, why not?" said Julia.

"Good luck with that," said David.

1,219,881.

Patented Mar. 20, 1917.

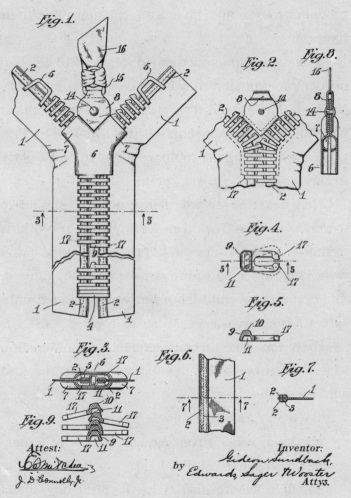

Fig.1.

Fig.2.

Fig.8.

Fig.4.

Fig.5.

Fig.3.

Fig.6.

Fig.7.

Fig.9.

Attest:

Inventor:
Gideon Sundback,
by Edwards, Sager & Wooster
Attys.

It took three days for the *Carpathia* to get to New York City. The Flashback Four spent most of that time wandering around the deck, brainstorming other products they could invent and planning for their future.

Nobody would know them in New York. They had no identification, but they had a thousand dollars. As a group, they agreed to pretend they were orphans who had lost their parents on the *Titanic*. The first thing they would need to do would be to find a place to stay.

They talked about whether or not they should go to school in New York. Not all twelve-year-old kids went to school in those days. If the zipper idea didn't work out, they could always get jobs, they agreed. The first federal child labor law wasn't passed until 1916.

There was a bustle of excitement and anticipation when one of the other passengers spotted the first glimpse of land.

"It's New York City!" somebody shouted.

Word got passed around quickly and all the passengers rushed to the rail.

"I went to New York on a trip with my family when I was a little kid," David told the others as they squinted their eyes to see. "We went up to the top of the Empire State Building. And I had a hot dog on the street. That's all I remember."

"I don't think the Empire State Building was even built in 1912," Isabel said.

She was right. It would be nineteen years before the classic skyscraper would be completed. The New York skyline as they knew it didn't exist yet. In 1912, the tallest structure in the world was—believe it or not—the Eiffel Tower in Paris. They would be arriving to a different world.

"Look!" Julia suddenly shouted. "I see it!"

There it was, one of the most famous images in the world—the Statue of Liberty, holding her torch high in the sky. It was a beautiful thing.

A hush fell over the passengers at the rail of the *Carpathia*. Luke turned around to see the other passengers looking at it. Their eyes were filled with hope. Many of them had come to America for the freedom it offered. He and his friends would have freedom too— maybe more freedom than they really wanted.

It was raining slightly when the ship approached New York Harbor. Thanks to the recent invention of the wireless, the newspapers had been alerted about what happened to the *Titanic*. So the whole world knew about it. As a result, the waters around Pier 54 were swarming with rowboats full of reporters hoping to get exclusive interviews with the survivors.

"Did you see the iceberg?" one of them shouted through a megaphone.

"What happened to Mr. Astor?" asked another. "Is it true that he is dead?"

"Did you see people drowning?"

Photographers in the boats were jockeying for position to take the pictures that would appear in all the newspapers the next day. They fired off dozens of blinding magnesium flashes.

"Horrid vultures," one of the passengers grumbled. "Just horrid."

The sight of all those photographers gave Julia another idea.

"Y'know," she whispered to Luke, "I bet we could make a *fortune* selling that picture you took of the Titanic."

"We could," he replied, "if there was a way to get it out of the camera."

"Oh yeah," Julia said, disappointed. There were no digital cameras in 1912. There was no digital *anything* in 1912.

The newspapers would report that there were

thirty *thousand* people waiting to greet the *Carpathia* as it docked at Pier 54. That may have been an exaggeration, but the place was jammed. People were everywhere, waving, shouting, and crying. American flags were flying at half-mast to mourn the *Titanic* passengers who had lost their lives.

"I can't wait to see Mommy and Daddy," said a little girl on the *Carpathia* as she scanned the faces of the people below.

"We will start a new life in America," a Bulgarian man told his family.

"So will we," mumbled Julia.

Luke had been quiet as the ship pulled into New York Harbor. An idea had been bubbling up in his head, but he was reluctant to mention it until he had thought it through. Finally, as ropes were being tied to secure *Carpathia* to the pier, he decided to share it with the others.

"Guys," he said with excitement in his eyes, "I just got a great idea!"

"You're just trying to cheer us up, man," David replied. "I know you."

"No, listen," Luke said. "It just hit me. Miss Z is going to be down there with all those people."

"What?" said Isabel.

"She's down there!" Luke insisted. "She *has* to be."

"What do you mean?" asked David. "That makes no sense at all."

"Think about it," Luke told them. "She was texting us with the TTT, and suddenly it stopped working, right? She doesn't know it fell into the water. But when we stopped communicating, she must have figured we either went down with the *Titanic* or we got into a lifeboat, right? So put yourself in her shoes. She's going to try to bring us back. What would *you* do?"

"I'd go to New York," David replied.

"Right!" Luke said. "But not New York in the twenty-first century. That wouldn't do any good. She had to go to New York in 1912."

"So she'd use the Board to send herself here!" shouted Isabel. "Then she could use it to bring us back home!"

"Exactly!"

"But she told us she can't send us to the same place twice," Julia said. "Remember?"

"It's *not* the same place!" Luke told Julia. "She sent us to the middle of the Atlantic Ocean the first time. And that was four days ago."

"Luke is right!" Isabel exclaimed. "She's going to be there! We're going to be rescued!"

All four members of the Flashback Four were suddenly filled with hope as they looked over the railing to search the crowd below. There were thousands of faces down there.

"How will we find Miss Z?" asked Julia.

"We won't have to," Luke assured her. "She'll find *us*."

The gangplank was lowered and the passengers began lining up to get off the ship. First, a few people who needed medical attention were carried off in stretchers. Finally the line began to move forward and the Flashback Four made their way down the long gangplank.

Lists of the *Titanic*'s survivors had already appeared in the newspapers, but they were incomplete. Many of the people waiting at the dock had no idea whether their loved ones were alive or not. So when they finally saw their brothers, sisters, aunts, and uncles coming off the *Carpathia*, there was a huge outpouring of emotion. Entire families broke down in tears of happiness as they were reunited with loved ones.

As they walked down the gangplank, the Flashback Four scanned the sea of faces, looking for Miss Z.

"Is that her?" Isabel said excitedly, pointing to a lady sitting in a wheelchair.

"Nah, too old," said David.

"Miss Z might have sent somebody else to come get us," suggested Luke. "That would make sense."

"Maybe she sent Mrs. Vader," said Julia. "Keep an eye out for her."

"It could be *anybody* here," David said.

They reached the end of the gangplank and stepped onto solid ground for the first time in four days. The dock was filled with people, making it hard to move. The Flashback Four joined hands so they would not be separated. They made their way to one side, where it wasn't so crowded.

"Miss Z will be able to find us more easily after some of these people go home," Isabel said.

It had stopped raining. The Flashback Four continued to watch the crowd. Old-time cars spewing exhaust came and left the streets around Pier 54, taking passengers away. Some people got picked up by a horse and buggy. An hour went by.

"She must be here *somewhere*," Isabel said, continuing to scan the crowd left and right.

"Maybe she got caught in traffic," suggested Julia.

"There's no traffic!" David said, rolling his eyes. "She's using the Board to get here, remember?"

"Oh yeah."

Another hour passed. Every time a stranger walked in their direction and made eye contact, the Flashback Four got excited, thinking it could be the person who was coming to pick them up. But the person always walked away, going to greet somebody else.

Hopes were starting to fade.

By around four o'clock in the afternoon, the crowd had thinned out. Almost all of the passengers had been picked up. The reporters and photographers had left to go file their stories for the morning papers. The sun was dipping down in the sky. Soon it would be dark out.

"Where *is* she?" Luke asked impatiently as he paced back and forth.

A park bench on the dock was empty, so Luke, Isabel, Julia, and David went over and sat on it.

"Maybe she forgot about us," David said, his shoulders drooping.

"She didn't forget," Luke replied.

"Maybe she just doesn't care what happens to us," Isabel said sadly. "Maybe she's just not coming. I *knew* this whole thing was a mistake from the beginning."

Even Luke, always the optimist, didn't argue the point.

As the last of the other passengers left the dock

with their families, Luke, David, Isabel, and Julia sat silently on the bench looking out at the Statue of Liberty in New York Harbor, and wondered what their future would be.

EPILOGUE

WHAT WILL HAPPEN TO THE FLASHBACK FOUR? Will they ever be picked up and returned to Boston in the present day? Or will they live the rest of their lives a century in the past? And most importantly, will they invent the zipper?

You'll have to wait for the *next* Flashback Four adventure to find out.

FACTS & FICTIONS

Everything in this book is true, except for the stuff I made up. It's only fair to tell you which is which.

First, the made-up stuff. The Flashback Four, Miss Z, and Mrs. Vader do *not* exist. There's no such thing as a smartboard that enables people to travel through time. At least not yet.

The *Titanic*, of course, did exist. Lots of ships have sunk throughout history, and some suffered more casualties. But none was as famous as the *Titanic*.

People who grew up during this millennium remember September 11. People who grew up in the 1960s remember the Kennedy assassination. People who grew up in the 1940s remember Pearl Harbor. And people who were growing up in 1912 would always remember where they were when they heard the *Titanic* had sunk.

Just about everything in this book about the *Titanic*—the names, dates, times, locations, statistics—is true. I did the research by reading many of the hundreds of books that have been written on the subject. Two were especially helpful: *A Night to Remember* by Walter Lord and *The Story of the Titanic as Told by Its Survivors* by Jack Winocour. If you're fascinated by the *Titanic*—as so many people are—there's lots more information about it. Go to your local library. Google it. There's tons of stuff online.

And of course, watch the 1997 movie *Titanic* if you haven't already seen it. By the way, it cost more money to make that movie than it cost to build the original ship!

Part of the story of the *Titanic* that did *not* fit in this book was what happened after the tragedy was over. An investigation was held, and as a result many things were done to make ships safer. They were built with double hulls and bigger bulkheads. They were required to have wireless communication equipment. The International Conference on the Safety of Life at Sea created a system to observe and track the path of icebergs. And of course, ships were required to carry enough lifeboats to hold all the passengers and crew.

Today, some cruise ships are twice the size of *Titanic*, and they're much safer.

A lot of people are to blame for the tragedy of the *Titanic*, but nobody was ever arrested or jailed for it. It was never determined who made the decision to use iron rivets instead of steel, or who decided sixteen lifeboats was enough, or who misplaced the ship's only pair of binoculars.

Captain Smith went down with the ship, and his body was never found.

The lookout who first spotted the iceberg seconds before the collision actually survived. His name was Frederick Fleet. He would commit suicide, but that was many years later (1965), and it appeared to have nothing to do with the *Titanic* tragedy.

John Jacob Astor's body was one of the 306 found floating in the water after *Titanic* went under. The initials on his shirt collar, his jewelry, and $2,440 in his pocket were used to identify him. His young wife, Madeleine survived, and gave birth to a son four months later. She named him John Jacob. Madeleine would have inherited five million dollars if she had remained single, but she gave it up when she fell in love with a childhood friend and married him. She had two more children and died from a heart ailment in 1940 at age forty-six. John Jacob died in 1992.

Isidor Straus's body was recovered, but his loving wife, Ida, was never found.

For decades after it went under, treasure hunters searched for the wreck of the *Titanic*. It sat undisturbed on the ocean floor for seventy-three years. Then, on September 1, 1985, oceanographer Bob Ballard finally discovered it—ten miles from where it had been thought to be. It was Ballard who confirmed what some witnesses had reported—that the *Titanic* had broken into two pieces before it sank.

Most people don't know that the *Carpathia*, the ship that rushed to rescue the *Titanic* survivors, *also* met with a sad ending. In July of 1918, near the end of World War I, it was torpedoed and sunk by a German submarine. For more than eighty years, it also sat undiscovered at the bottom of the Atlantic Ocean. Then, in 2000, it was discovered, 120 miles west of Ireland.

Now the story of the *Titanic* is beginning to fade from memory. In 2009, the last survivor of the ship passed away. Her name was Millvina Dean. She was nine weeks old when the Titanic sank, and ninety-seven when she died.

But the sad story of the *Titanic* continues to capture our imaginations, and every few years it comes back for the next generation to find, and to remind us of the limits of technology and the power of Mother Nature.

ABOUT THE AUTHOR

Besides Flashback Four, Dan Gutman is the author of The Genius Files, My Weird School, Rappy the Raptor, the Baseball Card Adventures, and many other books for young readers. He lives in New York City with his wife, Nina.